THE SCRY'S THE LIMIT

ADA BELL

EMPRESS BOOKS

Just when Aly thinks she understands her psychic powers, a new mystery puts them to the test.

Life in Shady Grove is looking up. Aly's excited to start classes at Maloney College, she loves her job, and her unrequited crush might be starting to turn into an actual flirtation. If only she could figure out how her sister-in-law died and help her brother move on, everything would be awesome. Then, Aly's academic advisor and favorite professor turns up dead.

Professor Zimm was one of the school's most beloved teachers. Who would want to kill her? The colleague who could make tenure in her absence? The athlete who resents having to retake the class? The rich girl who's determined to get an A at all costs? There's no shortage of suspects, but Aly's running out of time to find the killer before they find her.

ALSO BY ADA BELL

Shady Grove Psychic Mysteries

Mystic Pieces

The Scry's the Limit

Sight Seering

Mystic Treasure (Book 3.5)

Seer Today, Gone Tomorrow

The Pie in the Scry

Mystic Persons

To Sara

*I forgot to get you a birthday present
so this will have to do.*

CHAPTER ONE

YOU REALLY HAD to hand it to the maker of this blindfold: no matter how I craned my neck, I couldn't see a thing. Butter-flies hammered out a rhythm against the inside of my stomach. Not even my first day on the job had brought me as much anxiety as these tests my boss arranged. I took a deep breath, steadying my nerves as always by mentally reciting the elements of the periodic table.

Element twenty-three was vanadium. Element twenty-four was chromium.

"Are you ready, Aly?" My boss's voice came from directly in front of me, so close I could have reached out and touched her. Which was precisely the point: I'd come to the store to test my powers.

Missing Pieces was an antique shop that helped people find the "new to them" things they didn't know they needed. In reality, Olive Green had a psychic ability that allowed her to touch an object and get a vision of its "true owner." She made matches based on those impressions, which is why the store rarely got returns or exchanges. People adored their purchases.

The first time I entered this store, an irresistible sensation pulled me toward a gorgeous opal ring. When I put it on, I saw the death of the prior owner. Didn't just see it. I felt the car accident. Considering it had been my first vision ever—and, as a biology major, I prided myself on logical thinking—it was safe to say that wasn't my finest moment. I couldn't wrap my head around the possibility of psychics even existing, much less that I might be one. But Olive and I had come a long way, and we'd been doing experiments all morning. Hence the blindfold.

Something light touched my fingertips. Distracted by my thoughts, I wasn't prepared. The item started to roll away, and without thinking, I grabbed it. Instantly, my world shifted.

A scroll of parchment lay in front of me. Tiny, cramped writing filled the surface, the black ink glistening. In my right hand, I held a long, feathered quill. An open ink pot sat on the large wooden table before me. Men filled the room.

Picking up the parchment in one hand, I adjusted my bifocals and squinted at the top line. "We hold these truths to be self-evident..."

With an excited squeak, I dropped the pen. The feeling of it hitting my toe through my boot told me the world had returned to normal. Alas, my blindfold had replaced the wire-rimmed glasses.

Before Olive could say a word, I asked, "You have one of the original pens used to sign the Declaration of Independence? Why didn't you tell me? Kevin would love this!" My brother was a lawyer, excited by all things legal and boring. Er, I mean…No, I meant that pretty much how it sounded.

Her voice held a trace of amusement. "Because that's not for Kevin."

"Right. Duh."

"I take it you had a vision, then?"

"Yes! But I don't feel like it counts. I grabbed the pen so I wouldn't drop it, but then I was basically holding it the way someone would use it to write."

My gift didn't work like hers. You could hand me a hundred items, and I wouldn't have any idea who the owner was unless it came with a name tag. Instead, sometimes I saw snippets of important events in a person's life. Most often deaths, so far, but other life-altering moments, too. Like a wedding proposal once. That was nice.

"Sorry about that," Olive said. "Next time, I'll make sure you're ready."

"I'm ready. Let's keep going."

"Okay. This isn't something you'd use holding it like a pen, so go ahead and grip as tight as you want."

She set something cool on my palm. I closed my fingers around the item, trying to focus on it with my mind. The weight of the object told me it was probably metal, but the whole point of this exercise was to avoid using my five senses. I needed to learn to choose when and where to trigger a vision rather than having them come to me at inopportune moments.

Nothing was happening, so I put my hands together, allowing myself to determine what I held. Flat, smooth, cool to the touch. Some kind of jewelry. In a circle. Olive had given me a bracelet, but that's not what we wanted to find out.

To date, I'd only been able to get impressions from objects by using them in the intended manner. Sometimes that turned awkward, so Olive was trying to help me learn to channel my energy in another way. Thus far, we'd had zero luck, but we kept working on it.

"Close your eyes. Concentrate." The sound of my boss's voice soothed me as I put all of my attention into the object. "Relax, Aly. Steam is rising out of your ears."

Okay, maybe Olive's voice wasn't as soothing as I thought. "I'm trying. Really."

"I know, I know. You're making progress."

"Hold on. That's metaphorical steam, right?" Here in Shady Grove, you never could be sure.

"Yes, dear," she said. "What do you see?"

Nothing. Nada. Zip. Zilch.

Instead of admitting defeat, I slid the bracelet over my left hand. Immediately, everything shifted. The ever-present ticking clock of the store faded away.

A woman's rich, full singing voice filled my ears. An audience appeared in front of my eyes, and I looked down to find my feet resting on a wooden stage. A shimmering pink gown came into view. Cotton candy pink high heels. My matching fingernails clutched a microphone. The singing came from within me.

With a sigh, I removed the bracelet and the blindfold. "I saw someone performing. Great voice, definitely not mine."

As my eyes adjusted to the light, Olive's kind face and dark blue eyes swam into focus. As usual, she wore her long, dark hair pulled back into a low bun. Today, she regarded me the same way teachers looked at an insolent pupil. For a moment, I felt about three years old. But when she spoke, her voice was kind.

"The bracelet belonged to a performer. We're making progress."

"Not really," I grumbled. "I had to put the bracelet on before I saw anything. At this rate, I'll never find out who killed Katrina."

A little over a year ago, my older brother came home from work to find his wife dead, the house unlocked, and no one in sight but their then two-year-old son. Police found signs of a struggle and determined that Katrina had been killed, but no suspects had ever been found.

Kevin sold their fancy McMansion outside New York City and moved Kyle north to Shady Grove, where I joined them to help out. To date, my assistance had been limited to providing child care, but when I discovered my powers, I resolved to find out what happened. Kevin deserved to know the truth.

Unfortunately, I wasn't having much luck. This was the fifth object Olive had handed me in the past hour, and while I'd triggered a vision with two of them, it was only because I used the objects, albeit one of them unintentionally.

"Relax. You've only known about your powers for what? Less than a month?" When I nodded sheepishly, Olive continued, "We'll figure this out. One thing at a time. For now, the good news is, you triggered two visions without seeing what you were using. That's progress. I promise."

"I know. Thanks." Something tickled the back of my mind. "Oh! Have you had any luck finding Katrina's stuff?"

Olive clucked her tongue sympathetically. "I'm sorry, dear. Nothing so far."

Before moving, Kevin gave away or donated most of his wife's personal belongings, finding it too painful to see the reminders. It was tough to get a reading when all I had was household items people had been using for over a year—including me. For the past couple of weeks, Olive had been using her contacts to try to find any items my brother pawned or donated before moving here. So far, she'd come up short.

"It's okay. We always knew it was a long shot. I'll keep searching the house."

"And I'll keep asking around." Olive gestured at the blindfold on the table between us. "Do you want to try again?"

I shook my head. "Thanks, but I've got to go. Classes start in less than an hour. I can't be late on my first day."

"That's right. You're going to learn all the things and become a brilliant psychic scientist."

I beamed at her. "All part of my master plan to save the world."

"If anyone can do it, you can."

The jingling bell over the door interrupted me, and I turned to find a hulking black overcoat, topped with a gray scarf and a matching hat. Sunglasses covered the person's eyes, leaving me nothing but a nose from which to guess the newcomer's identity.

My boss had no such dilemma.

"Sam!" She rushed toward the door with her arms stretched wide.

My heart leaped into my throat. Sam? Here?

Olive's son was in his early twenties, one of the best-looking guys I'd ever met, and completely unaware of the effect he had on me. He lived in New York City, was studying to be an accountant, and barely knew I was alive, but once I worked up the nerve to have a conversation with him about anything other than his mother, everything would change.

Olive didn't know I'd had an enormous crush on her son from the moment we'd met. Or maybe she did. Her gifts weren't entirely clear to me. Not that it mattered: Sam and I lived in different parts of the state. Our paths didn't cross much, an annoying fact that made it difficult for me to figure out how to get him to fall in love with me.

"Hey, Sam," I said as he started peeling off the outerwear. My voice came out in a squeak. So much for acting cool to keep my feelings secret. "I didn't know you were coming."

"Oh, I'm sure I mentioned it," Olive said. "Someone accidentally started a fire in his dorm, so he's doing remote classes for a week or so until it's safe to go back."

No, she didn't. You don't forget things like getting to spend time with the man you plan to marry. But it wasn't worth arguing with her.

A week! Seven days I might get to see Sam before he left town. Element seven was nitrogen. Highly explosive, just like our chemistry.

Going through the elements usually calmed me. Now, my thoughts sent my pulse racing even more.

"Hey, Aly," Sam said. "Good to see you. Are you okay?"

"Sorry." Blinking several times, I shook my head. "I'm fine. I just realized that if I don't leave now, I'm going to be late for my first day."

"Why is your first day on Thursday?" Sam asked.

"Snow," I said.

He nodded knowingly. Unexpected snow days were just part of life in New York.

"Only you would be sad about missing a day of school," Olive said.

"Aly's not the only one." Sam smiled at me, and my stomach flip-flopped. "Anyway, enjoy. I'll see you later today?"

"Tomorrow. I've got four classes today, and then Kyle duty."

As I waved goodbye, I resisted the urge to point out all the other things Sam and I had in common. It didn't matter. Until I got my powers under control, I didn't have any business worrying about my personal life.

CHAPTER TWO

UNLIKE PRETTY MUCH everyone else on the planet, the start of a new semester made me giddy. I loved the excitement of setting up and organizing folders on my hard drive, creating blank documents and files for each class, just waiting to be filled with knowledge.

Okay, yes, I was a nerd. Sometimes I thought the universe gave me psychic powers to balance out my total lack of cool. After all, my abilities never materialized until my twenty-first birthday, by which time my "nerd" status had solidified like coal getting pressed into diamonds. Science lover? Check. Math aficionado? Check? No dates in about a year? Check. Voluntarily spends all her time with a three-year-old? Check.

Not that having random visions did much to improve my cool factor. Especially since hardly anyone knew.

For the forty-seventh time, I reviewed my course load in my head. Everything happened in the same building, which helped. First molecular biology, then physics, organic chemistry, and cellular biology. These were all third-year courses; I'd gotten my associate's degree in California before moving out here.

About fifteen minutes before class started, I arrived at

Maloney College, turning my new-to-me blue Prius into the parking lot by the science building. The five-year-old car wasn't exactly sexy, but it was environmentally friendly and had plenty of room in the back for Kyle's car seat. The car seat space and safety ratings were crucial since current laws suggested my nephew would need the thing until he got his own license.

Driving a used car terrified me, to be honest. What if I got a vision of the former owner while headed down the Northway going seventy miles an hour? But I wasn't ready to hang up my driver's license forever at the age of twenty-one, and I couldn't afford a new vehicle on a part-time retail salary. Instead, I'd begged our next-door neighbor, whose daughter owned the local magic shop, to help me do a cleansing. So far, so good.

A spot opened up about halfway down the aisle, and I moved toward it, happy everything was proceeding on schedule. I should have time to park, hit the coffee shop, and slide into my seat before the rest of the students arrived. Then, as I swerved left to prepare for my turn, a tiny red blur zipped out of nowhere and screeched around me.

I slammed on the brakes, hardly daring to believe my eyes. The car halted, throwing me forward into the steering wheel. There was a car in my spot! A tiny vintage red sports car with license plate "QnTiff." Ugh.

For a long moment, I sat there, blinking. While I watched, a girl—presumably Tiff—with long black braids down her back exited the car and walked around to the trunk. She smirked at me as she grabbed a bright red backpack, slung it onto her back, and started trotting toward campus.

She stole my spot! And she *knew it*. Ugh. What was wrong with people?

With a groan of frustration, I moved toward the back of the lot, hoping something closer would open up. The parking lot stretched nearly half a mile, so a space at the far end would cost me my piping hot latte. Maybe this morning wasn't going so well after all.

Five minutes later, I pulled into an empty spot nowhere near my classroom and braced myself before opening the car door. The February morning air was freezing, of course, but sunny. The kind of beautiful crisp weather that tricked me into racing outside in my jammies one morning not long after I'd moved here. That's a mistake you only made once. Growing up in Sacramento, California, sun meant warmth, even in December. In Shady Grove, New York? Not so much.

With a shiver, I took off across the lot. No time for coffee, but with luck I'd still make it to my seat before the professor arrived. Nothing made a worse impression than being late on the first day.

It didn't take long to find my classroom, because I'd spent ten minutes memorizing the map the night before like a good nerd. I'd also scoped out the science building when I came to campus to buy my books.

By the time I finally arrived, only a handful of desks remained empty. Luckily, one was in the front of the room, right where I liked to be. I paused in the doorway to catch my breath.

"Excuse me!" The high-pitched voice came from behind me, but the owner didn't stay there. A pair of braids swished past me into the room. The girl who had stolen my parking spot entered, holding the latte I would currently be drinking if she hadn't made me late.

I realized her intention a split second too late. Moving as quickly as I could, I headed for the open seat. My seat.

With two steps to go, the girl stopped, turned, and plopped her latte onto the wooden surface. Maybe I could still—nope.

QnTiff sat and looked up at me, still wearing that smirk from the parking lot. "Did you need something?"

Sometimes, it would be nice if my psychic ability with

objects included the ability to throw them with my mind. Or with any accuracy using my arms. Alas, it did not. I swallowed back a snotty reply, shook my head, and glared at the two remaining empty seats, both located in the back row. Seats for people who wanted to hide, not shine. And for people who didn't care enough to show up on time.

Most of the other students scrolled on their phones. In stark contrast, the girl who stole my space—and my seat!—sat ramrod straight, hands folded on the desk in front of her, staring at the blackboard like she was trying to bore holes in it with her eyes. Heck, maybe she could do that. My horizons had been broadened significantly in the past few weeks.

Now that she'd removed her coat, she wore a white shirt buttoned to her chin. Combined with the hair, her overall look made me wonder if Little House on the Prairie was getting a reboot. Hopefully without the racism.

A hand on my arm jolted me out of my examination. I looked from red fingernails painted with lightning bolts up into Professor Zimm's smiling face. Nice. She had fun nails the first time we met, too. My own nails were short and completely uninteresting. Maybe I should get a manicure before visiting her office hours. Give us something to talk about. Or, you know, we could talk science.

She was a tall woman in her mid-fifties, with shoulder-length blonde hair. A pair of square purple glasses perched on the end of her long nose, and her full lips stretched into a contagious smile. She had unusually shiny teeth, which wasn't the kind of thing I'd normally notice, but they blinded me.

"Good morning. Are you ready to take your seat? Class starts in a few minutes."

I stammered out an apology and headed down the row, embarrassed to be singled out on the first day.

"Hey, I remember you." A good-looking guy with smiling

brown eyes and dark blond hair looked up as I slid into the seat next to him.

It took a minute to realize that why he looked familiar. We'd met in the parking lot when I came to campus to buy books. I remembered him largely because he'd been walking around in a tank top and basketball shorts in the middle of January. Also because he'd taught my three-year-old nephew the word "murda." Good times.

I racked my brain to come up with his name. "Hi. Brad, right?"

"And you're Aly. Your nephew likes basketball."

The fact that he remembered brought a smile to my face. "Kyle likes all kinds of ball, but yes. How are you? I'm excited about this class."

"Eh. It's not so great."

His comment piqued my interest. This wasn't one of the general education requirements, so why sign up if he wasn't interested? Few people took molecular biology for kicks.

"Oh, yeah? How do you know?"

"Took it last semester. Zimm flunked me."

A sympathetic sound escaped me. "Oh, no! What happened?"

"No big. I missed a few classes. Apparently that violated her 'attendance policy.'" He made air quotes with his hands before flopping back in his chair and crossing his legs, smacking the desk in front of him with one foot. When the guy sitting there turned around, Brad offered a shrug and a half nod. His demeanor made me wonder how many classes constituted "a few".

Before I could ask, Professor Zimm turned around from the whiteboard where she had been writing and addressed the class.

"Good morning, class! My name is Tabitha Zimm. Most of my students and TAs call me Tabby. Some of them call me 'Crabby Tabby,' and they think I don't know it."

Everyone chuckled.

She smiled and waved one hand dismissively. "It's okay. We're all crabby sometimes. Especially when our experiments don't work out. But that's neither here nor there. Speaking of experiments, You've all signed up to take Molecular Biology I. This is usually the point where someone scrambles out of the class in a panic, so I want to give you a chance to verify you're in the right place before I move onto the syllabus. Introduction to Geology is across the hall."

No one moved. Well, Brad tilted his head forward like he was nodding off, but that was it. The rest of the class seemed as riveted by Professor Zimm as I was. (I couldn't imagine calling her Tabby or even Tabitha.)

We'd met once before, the same day I met Brad, and I'd been instantly drawn to her positive energy. As she described the class we'd be taking, her enthusiasm for the subject made me like her even more. Then she took roll, cementing my love for her forever.

"Reynolds, Alu—Aly?"

In a thousand years, I would never forgive my parents for naming me Aluminum. It didn't matter that they loved science, or that aluminum was the thirteenth element of the periodic table, and I'd been born on the thirteenth of January. But Professor Zimm remembered our conversation about it in the bookstore, and she'd used my preferred nickname instead.

Brad gave me a funny look after responding to his name. "What did she call you?"

"Aly," I whispered. He'd get no more out of me.

He shrugged and went back to playing on his phone while Professor Zimm finished up the roll call. Part of me desperately wanted to point out that paying attention could help him avoid having to take the class a third time, but I kept my mouth shut. The last thing I wanted was for Murda Boy to ask me to tutor him.

After Brad's comment, I double-checked the attendance policy. Failing a class for something completely avoidable would make me so mad. No need to worry, though—Professor Zimm allowed people to miss as many classes as necessary with a valid excuse. Only unexcused absences were limited—to four. I didn't see any reason to skip class for two weeks without talking to her about it or getting a doctor's note, so I'd be fine. Maybe Brad didn't consider molecular biology to be a priority, but I did.

She finished reading the syllabus, then paused and clapped her hands. "You'll all be delighted to hear that for our first assignment, we're going to do a group project!"

Someone groaned loudly. Without seeing who it was, I whole-heartedly agreed with them. The excitement on the professor's face was almost enough to make me not roll my eyes, but not quite. Group projects were the worst. The only people who liked them were those who could coast on the work done by their "partners", narcissists, and sadistic professors. Maybe I should reevaluate my assessment of her character.

"Oh, don't look at me like that. This one will be fun, I promise."

As she talked about the project requirements, which involved growing yeast cultures and checking to see if UV light affected the cells, I let my eyes travel around the room without moving my head. Trying to get a look at prospective partners without making eye contact. In my peripheral vision, Brad waved to get my attention, but he was one of the last people I wanted to work with. Sure, he seemed nice enough. But he also was the stereotypical jock, and the fact that he'd already failed this class once combined with his total disdain for the professor gave me zero confidence in his willingness to work hard. I had no intention of carrying my study partners through this class. Got enough of that in high school, thank you very much.

"Now, since this is the first day, I assigned your groups before class to speed things along," Professor Zimm said. "You'll be working in teams of three. When I say your name, raise your hand so the other members of your group can find you."

It didn't take long for me to figure out she was going down the roster alphabetically, especially since she'd just finished calling roll. Since "R" wouldn't come up for a while, I allowed myself to relax until I heard her say "Tiffaneigh Pratt."

Queen Tiff. The horrible girl at the front of the room shot her hand into the air. She looked around the room smugly, as if raising her hand when called required enormous talent.

Oh, no. Not her. Anyone but her.

As expected, the next name on the list was "Aly Reynolds." I lifted my palm in the barest of acknowledgments, and our eyes met. Tiffaneigh gave me a thin smile that told me she was absolutely sizing me up to determine whether I'd let her be the group leader. I glared back at her, not giving anything away. As long as I could avoid anything resembling public speaking, I didn't care what my role was. I'd do whatever it took to help us get a good grade, but she could be the face of the project.

I was so busy checking out the first member of my group, I almost didn't hear the next name called. "Bradley Stevens."

Wonderful.

"Guess you have to give me your number now," Brad whispered beside me.

This time, I didn't even bother to conceal my eye roll. But since he was right, I wrote it on a corner of paper ripped from my planner and handed it to him with my SocialApp information.

My phone rang, taking my attention away from Brad's winking. Ugh. I wasn't sure which annoyed me more. Who called people anymore? I didn't recognize the number, but the area code was Shady Grove. Good thing the phone was on silent, but it vibrated so loudly in my bag, everyone turned to look at me.

"Sorry," I said, averting my eyes.

"It's okay, Aly," Professor Zimm said. "You wouldn't be the first person to fake an emergency to get out of a group assignment."

Everyone laughed, and she went back to announcing the last two groups. I hit the red button to send the call away. A moment later, it buzzed again with a voicemail. Seriously? Was the call from 1995?

When Professor Zimm dismissed the class, I got my answer. Three notifications showed on my screen: a missed call, a voice mail, and a text message. All of a sudden, a chill went down my spine. What if something happened to Kyle? The school's number should be saved in my Contacts, but what if they had another line I didn't know about?

Trying not to panic, I clicked to open the texts. The first one that popped up was from Brad, sending me his number so we could talk about the assignment. I whisked it away. Then the words on my screen sent a different kind of tremor through me.

Aly, it's Mary Towne. Katrina's sister. We need to talk.

CHAPTER THREE

MARY TOWNE. Katrina's sister had my number. And a local area code. Did that mean she was in town? She'd checked into a hotel or something?

As much as I hated to talk on the phone, some rules were meant to be broken. I tapped her number while walking down the hall toward my next class. A beep informed me that the call failed. Twice. Three times. Argh! No bars inside this part of the building for some reason. Stupid technology.

Eight minutes until my next class. About forty feet to get outside, and why was I even pretending to think about this? My hand was pushing the door open before I even finished the thought. Yes, I'd probably wind up in the last row again, but worth it. As long as that Tiffaneigh girl didn't get the last good seat.

My call went directly to voice mail, darn it. Either Mary had the good sense to put her phone on Do Not Disturb when she was busy, or she'd turned it off. Six minutes to go. I sent a quick text.

Sorry I missed you. I'm in class. Next break at 3. Call me then?

She hadn't replied by the time I made it back inside, which meant I unfortunately spent half of physics checking my phone under the desk. This was never going to work. Thankfully, the professor didn't seem to notice my distraction. And he didn't give us a group project, so yay.

My phone remained quiet, so I bolted outside at the next opportunity. Nothing. I called Mary again, but no dice. Why would she call and leave me a message if she wasn't going to answer when I called back? Grr.

Swallowing a groan of frustration, I forced myself to turn the device off for my last two classes.

By the time my biology seminar ended, I was chomping at the bit. I bolted out of the room so fast, I could have qualified at the race track. I needn't have bothered: the low battery alert popped up on my screen as my finger hovered over the call button. Could I make it to my car charger before it died? Maybe, but I'd be too stressed to focus on the conversation.

Reason caught hold of me somewhere between the classroom and the power cord in my car. Before I called Mary yet again, I needed to talk to Kevin. Over the past year, my older brother had become my closest friend, my confidant for everything—well, almost. He still didn't know about my powers.

All the way home, I wondered what Katrina's sister could possibly have to say about my sister-in-law's death. What was Mary doing in Shady Grove after all this time? Katrina died more than a year ago, and Mary had barely spoken to me at the funeral. Not that I blamed her. She was one of the bereaved, and I was the other bereaved's kid sister, occupied with a two-year-old most of the time. With a nine-year age gap between me and Kevin, we hadn't been close, and I'd only met Katrina a couple of times.

I waited until dinner was on the table and Kyle dove into his dinosaur nuggets before I broached the subject. (It had been my turn to cook.) "Hey, Kevin, did you know Mary's in town?"

He blinked several times. "Katrina's sister Mary? Not specifically, but I'm not surprised. She lives in Willow Falls."

This time I was the one taken aback. "Hold up. She lives nearby, and we haven't seen or talked to her in over a year. Why not?"

"Aunt Mary!" Kyle said. Apparently, he wasn't as into his food as I thought. "Aunt Mary fun."

"You know your aunt?" I asked him.

Around a mouthful of macaroni, he said, "We swing."

"Mary used to take him to the playground when she visited at the old house. I didn't think he'd remember."

"So why is she calling me from a Shady Grove number?"

"Shady Grove and Willow Falls have the same area code," he reminded me.

Right. Along with half the upper part of the state. After growing up in a big-ish city, I tended to forget that our area code stretched up to the Canadian border. "Why didn't you ever mention her?"

"I thought you knew," he said. "That's one reason I picked Shady Grove. I wanted Kyle to know his mother's family, and Mary was her closest relative. Their father took off when they were kids, and their mother died ten years ago."

Ouch. Poor Katrina. Her father hadn't even been at her funeral, as far as I knew. "Okay, that makes sense. Why haven't we seen or heard from her since then? Why haven't you invited her over? It would be great for Kyle to spend more time with his mother's sister. Especially since he apparently likes her."

Between us, Kyle said, "Call Aunt Mary?"

"Not now, Buddy." Kevin sighed and shook his head. "Mary didn't do well after Katrina's death. She had a minor breakdown. Spent time in rehab. I hadn't heard that she was out, but I honestly didn't check. She never contacted me."

"Don't you think it's weird that she would call me instead of you?"

He shook his head. "Actually no. She, uh…always blamed me for what happened."

Poor guy. He blamed himself, too, I knew it. That was one reason I'd sworn to find out what happened. We needed to know the truth so Kevin could move on.

Unfortunately, as badly as I wanted to hop in my car and drive straight to Willow Falls, I had other plans for this evening. I shot off another text before brushing my teeth and running a comb through my hair, hoping to get a response from Mary before heading out the door. No such luck. My screen remained dark, other than the forty-seven new messages from Tiffaneigh. Twenty minutes later, I arrived at Brad's house to discuss the group project.

At first, I'd questioned the need to start work immediately. Not because I had other plans or anything. Kevin had a book club meeting, so I'd hoped to get time to search the basement for any clue about what happened to my sister-in-law.

Unfortunately, Tiffaneigh insisted we needed to get started as soon as possible, and Brad had a basketball game in Rochester on Saturday. They both had class tomorrow morning, and our babysitter wasn't free Friday night. I didn't have a better excuse for asking to put things off than "I want to dig through my basement," and my grade depended on these two, so I'd asked Mrs. Patel to watch Kyle and arrived at the address provided at seven o'clock on the dot.

Brad lived in the type of house that came straight out of a fairy tale. The white colonial had turrets in the front, bay windows, and a peaked roof. The mailbox looked like a gingerbread house, candy and all. It didn't fit him even a little bit, but I suddenly wondered if his mother had her clothes sewn by talking mice.

A glance at the spacious driveway told me Tiffaneigh had already arrived, so I parked behind her stupid, shiny red Mustang and climbed the porch steps.

Brad opened the front door before I even finished knocking. "Good thing you're here. Tiffaneigh hasn't let me say a word since she arrived."

I stifled the urge to laugh as I followed him through the house to the kitchen. Two tablets sat on the large wooden table, with papers strewn across every available inch of the surface. Surprised, I checked the time on the stove. "Am I late?"

"No, I'm always fifteen minutes early," Tiffaneigh said.

"I wasn't even home when she got here," Brad said. "She was sitting on the doorstep. I'm lucky she didn't break in."

Her face turned red in a way that made me suspect Tiffaneigh may have tried to gain entrance on her own. Seeing my gaze, she became very absorbed in something written on her tablet. To deflect, I asked Brad for something to drink. He suggested beer with a wink. Ick.

Olive had warned me not long after discovering my powers that alcohol could have an impact on how they affected me. Or that my new powers might do something to the way alcohol got processed by my system. Either way, I hadn't had time to experiment yet since I'd only turned twenty-one in January. Brad's house during a group project wasn't the place to start.

I went with water.

The project itself wasn't difficult. We'd be growing cell cultures, measuring them for different qualities, and then tracking the results. To be honest, it was something I could have done myself. That boded well, since Brad acted like he couldn't bother to do anything other than provide a place to house the experiment. Fine with me—yeast cultures and three-year-olds didn't mix.

"Did you do this last semester?" I asked Brad.

He shook his head. "No. It wasn't assigned."

Tiffaneigh wrinkled her nose. "What are you talking about? OMG, did you fail this class once?" She said the word "fail" like it physically pained her to spit it out. I would've laughed if I hadn't felt bad about inadvertently revealing Brad's embarrassment. "If this project brings down my GPA—"

I put my hand on her arm. "Calm down. It's one project."

"One project where Professor Zimm put me with someone who's going to screw us over by not doing the work! Oh, I could kill her."

The tips of his ears turned pink. "Not failed, exactly. I thought I'd dropped, so I didn't show up. Uh…at all."

Interesting. Not what he'd told me earlier. If he'd dropped, how did he know there was no group project? It could've been assigned later.

Tiffaneigh said, "You know you can get that removed, right? So it doesn't mess up your GPA. You just need to do a petition."

"Yeah. I did that my freshman year after Coach threatened to kick me off the team if my grades didn't improve. I asked her to let me do extra credit, but she said no."

"Ugh." She snorted in disgust. "What a witch."

"Yeah."

They both looked at me, but I didn't have it in me to agree. I liked Professor Zimm, and I looked forward to working with her throughout the year. I'd already planned to ask if she needed a TA for the summer semester. I'd love to help out in her lower-level chemistry labs. Maybe run some experiments on myself.

Er, wait. I didn't say that.

Pulling my tablet out of my bag, I settled into a chair. "Should we get started?"

"I made a few notes based on the reading." Tiffaneigh pulled a thick stack of papers from her bag, tagged with different colored paperclips and about a million of those tiny paper flags sticking out. Class had ended like six hours ago.

Brad's eyes bugged out, but he didn't say anything. My expression probably mirrored his. Tiffaneigh ignored us both and handed out stacks of paper, already chattering about her ideas.

The good news was, Tiffaneigh had done an incredibly thorough job of preparing us for this assignment. Better than I'd done myself, as much as I hated to admit it. So good, I suspected that she might have prepared it all before today. This didn't look like something thrown together in a few hours between other classes. If I wanted to keep up with our group alpha, I needed to up my game.

At least I knew enough about the material to nod along and ask questions. Brad looked like he wanted to go to sleep. The fifteenth time his eyes darted to his phone, I started to ask why he signed up for the class in the first place when he clearly didn't care. The rumble of an automatic garage door outside interrupted our session.

A moment later, a car door slammed, the familiar beep of a car alarm engaged, and a door swung into the kitchen.

"Mom! What did I tell you about borrowing my clothes?" Brad bellowed toward the opening. I cringed. Never could I imagine talking to my mother like that. Or anyone.

A sound of frustration came from the direction of what must be a mudroom. One foot stamped on the ground, then another. Then someone called, "Sorry. Your coat looks like mine."

"That's what you get for trying to pretend you're twenty. Did you at least put it back?"

"It's on the hook." A woman appeared in the doorway. She had to be Brad's mom, but I'd never have believed it looking at her. Unless she had him when she was like twelve. She looked like one of those perfect women you saw in magazines, hair shaved in the back, cut to frame her chin in front, a platinum blond found naturally on exactly no one. "Why, hello, girls. I'm Lacey Stevens, Brad's mom."

Brad introduced us, then said, "Where have you been? I thought you'd be home over an hour ago."

"Oh, you know how it is. One thing leads to another. Babette just goes on and on, and she doesn't even care that I'm freezing to death while she talks about her charity luncheon. I need to go take a shower to warm up. Why don't you order dinner?"

"Takeout again?" If I'd taken that tone with my parents, I might be going to bed hungry, but Lacey didn't appear to notice.

"Sorry. I promise I'll go shopping tomorrow. Girls, are you staying?"

A glance at the clock on the microwave told me it was nearly eight o'clock. People ate dinner this late? On purpose?

"I'd love to," Tiffaneigh said just as I replied, "I have to get going soon."

"Are you sure?" she asked.

"Yeah. Thanks for letting us work here. Your house is amazing."

"No problem," she said. "I love when Brad invites his friends over. Sometimes I think he's ashamed of me."

His cheeks turned red. "Of course I'm not—"

"He hates the way I tell everyone about his famous father who paid for this gorgeous house and then ditched us."

Tiffaneigh shot Brad a look. "Your dad's famous?"

He shrugged. "Not really."

"He's a hockey star!" Mrs. Stevens said. "He'll be in the Hall of Fame one day, I know it. We met when he played for the local minor league team. Before they moved away. By the time we got married, he had a multi-million-dollar, five-year deal in the NHL. Brad, you should be proud."

"That's so cool! I'm from California. I don't know anyone who plays hockey," I said.

"I prefer basketball," Brad muttered. "Dad didn't understand."

"We just wanted you to follow in his footsteps, dear," Mrs.

Stevens said. "Well, up until the part where he started sleeping with puck bunnies."

"I'm sorry," Tiffaneigh raised her hand. "He what?"

Glad she asked instead of me. Because, having never met Mr. Stevens, I didn't need to know what he was into.

"That's the term for hockey groupies," Brad told her.

"Did you even know hockey groupies were a thing?" Mrs. Stevens asked.

"Uh-no. I didn't," I said.

"Me, neither," Tiffaneigh chimed in.

"Listen to me go on," Mrs. Stevens said. "I don't want to distract you from your work. Bradley, you will get an A this time."

"I told you I'd handle it," Brad snapped. "You don't have to ride me."

"Don't talk to me like that!" his mother began.

"Oh, would you look at the time?" Tiffaneigh asked. All of a sudden, she looked desperate to leave.

At least I understood why Brad didn't invite friends over often.

Back in my car, I checked my phone, but Mary hadn't returned my text. Now it was too late to call her, darn it. I sent a second message, letting her know that I expected to be doing homework until midnight and could talk to her whenever she had a few minutes free. Crossing my fingers it was enough, I headed home to search my house for clues.

Every night for the past week, I'd been sneaking into the basement. Okay, I lived in the house, so I had a right to be in any room I wanted, but there was never much need to enter the storage room down there. It was tucked away beyond the washer/dryer, which I typically avoided as long as possible. But now, I dug through one box per night, searching in vain for anything belonging to Katrina. It was a slow, tedious process. At this point, I'd be ecstatic to find a used stick of gum.

Well, grossed out, but in a happy way.

As I pulled my car into the driveway, I breathed a sigh of relief to discover I'd beaten Kevin home. Rushing inside, I paid Mrs. Patel, tried to act natural while basically pushing her out the door, and raced to the basement.

There wasn't much time, but I could take a quick look around the basement storage area. There were only so many boxes down here. I had to be getting closer to finding something, right?

Wrong.

The first box I opened contained nothing but a supply of every type of power cord known to man. I couldn't even identify half the connection types I saw in there, but the word "Nintendo" stamped on one of the power boxes told me everything I needed to know. What was the point of keeping this stuff? Even if he woke up one day with a desperate desire to play Super Mario Bros. for the first time in twenty-five years, he'd be better off with an emulator.

After confirming there was nothing of interest, I crammed everything back into the box and shut the lid. It hadn't been sorted before; I wasn't doing it now.

On to box number two of the night. Box twenty-seven or so overall. Hopefully Kevin never noticed the dots I'd been leaving near the bottom of each one after I dug through it.

At first glance, there wasn't much of interest here, either. Some assorted books and exercise bands. Pieces I recognized from Halloween the year Kevin dressed as Sherlock Holmes. Then something glinted against the bottom. A silver key.

It could open anything: a gym locker, a filing cabinet, an old jewelry box. But something told me this key would lead me to answers. I grabbed it, taking a moment to examine the attached green ring. A big circle with the number seventy-eight stamped on one side.

Seventy-eight what? Did Kevin have some old motel room key? Ick.

I flipped the ring over, and my eyes widened. *Joey's Storage.*

There wasn't any place in town named Joey's Storage as far as I knew. And we had all this space here. No need for a storage unit. But if you wanted to store your dead wife's belongings somewhere that you didn't have to see the painful memories? A storage unit made a lot of sense.

After stuffing the key in my pocket, I pulled out my phone and searched for the company name. One point three million results. I added the name of the town where they used to live and searched again. Bingo.

Joey's Storage, located about five blocks from Kevin and Katrina's McMansion. One hundred units. Finally, I understood why I'd had so little luck finding anything of Katrina's to do a reading.

Suddenly, the light in the outer basement snapped on. The flick of the switch thundered in the silence. I jolted upright, jamming the key into a pocket of my leggings. My eyes darted around the room, but although some of the boxes were pretty large, none of them had room for me to climb inside. A stupid idea, anyway. I wasn't afraid of my brother.

The door opened, and Kevin appeared in the doorway. "Aly? What are you doing in here?"

CHAPTER FOUR

CAUGHT IN THE ACT. My mind raced as I tried to think of any way to explain why I'd be searching through my brother's private storage area. I'd brought nothing but clothes and books when I moved from California, so it's not like I could pretend to be looking for anything of my own. Not a lot of need for flip-flops in February here. Old family photos?

Element thirteen was aluminum. Like me. Element fourteen was silicon. Good thing I wasn't born a day late.

Dusting off my hands, I stood and moved away from the boxes. "I was just looking for a Halloween costume."

"Uh-huh. In February?"

"Well, not Halloween obviously. I'm, um, pledging a sorority."

"Right. And you're dressing as Sherlock Holmes for Rush Week?"

For a long moment, I stood under the intensity of his gaze, trying not to squirm. Part of me desperately wanted to go with the lie.

But no. I'd been keeping this huge secret for long enough. If I found out what happened to Katrina, I'd have to spill the whole truth anyway. If Kevin knew now, maybe he had something of his wife's to give me, which would save me a couple dozen hours of digging through old report cards and other assorted crap.

Before I could decide, he folded his arms, indicating that he would wait as long as necessary for me to tell him the truth. I caved. "I'm sorry, Kev. I know you told me to butt out, mind my own business. Part of me truly understands why you would say that. But another part...I can't. I need to know what happened to Katrina. Since you weren't willing to tell me anything about her murder, I thought I'd see what I could find out myself."

"By digging through my stuff?"

"By looking for something that belonged to Katrina."

"Why?"

"To see what it can tell me." I waited, saying nothing for a long time. Kevin didn't know about my gifts. I'd never found a way to tell him, partially because my discovery had been quickly followed by a murder that needed to be solved and partly because I worried he wouldn't believe me.

"I'm sorry we never talked about the details. It was just too painful." He took a deep breath. "I have no idea what happened to Katrina. I was at work when it happened, up to my eyeballs in jury selection for a big case. It was a nightmare. I'd barely been home in weeks preparing for the trial. I thought Katrina was home alone with Kyle, as usual. Her car was in the garage when I arrived home. But when I went inside, she was lying at the bottom of the stairs, neck broken."

A tear glistened at the corner of his eye. His pain was still so raw, the thought that Mary or anyone else might blame my brother made me see red.

"Where was Kyle?"

"On the landing," Kevin said. "We still had a baby gate then, and he stood there, clutching it. He' couldn't climb over. He was so quiet, so sad. I don't know if he saw anything, but I've prayed every day that he wouldn't remember. He can't talk about it. Nothing he said would be admitted into evidence at his age. Kyle doesn't need to carry that memory around inside him."

"And police ruled her death a homicide?"

"Yeah. The front door was locked, none of the neighbors saw anyone, but police said there were signs of a struggle." He shook his head. "They thought someone came to the door, maybe selling something. Came in, killed her, locked the knob from the inside, and left. I tried to explain that Katrina would never let a salesman in the house while caring for a two-year-old. It wasn't safe."

"Are you sure she was murdered?" I asked. "Maybe she slipped. Happens all the time."

"I don't think so." He averted his eyes. "But listen—what if she tripped over a toy on the stairs? Or what if she fell because she was distracted by Kyle's crying? Or because she was so tired?"

"Kevin." Reaching out, I put one hand on his arm. "Do you think Kyle had anything to do with Katrina's death?"

"No! Of course not. He was only two." My brother let out a sob. "I pushed Katrina into having kids. She said she might want them 'someday,' but I didn't want to wait. If she fell because she was tired and distracted, because she tripped over a toy, because of the baby…then it's my fault she's gone. It's easier to believe that someone came in and killed her, as horrible as that sounds."

My poor brother. The more he spoke, the more my heart broke for him. Kevin never wanted to talk about his wife's death because he felt responsible. My resolve to get my hands on something of Katrina's doubled. He deserved to know the truth, needed to forgive himself and move on. Most people in this situation would never know what happened without cameras, but I didn't need cameras. I just needed the right object.

"Why are you doing this?" Kevin asked. "Why now? Is it because of Mary?"

I couldn't tell him the truth: I was looking for clues now because now was when my psychic powers might help. Since I didn't know about them before, obviously, now had to be the time. But Kevin didn't believe in anything paranormal—he didn't even read fortune cookies. The truth would only make everything worse.

Instead, I grasped for the excuse he gave me. "Mary got me thinking. The police report had so little information. I guess I thought if I could see some of Katrina's old things, it might help me make sense of what happened."

It sounded bad even to my own ears, but he was either distracted enough not to notice the lie or he decided to let it go.

"I don't have anything of Katrina's. She's gone. I don't need to know what happened."

That didn't make any sense to me. His wife died and he didn't care how? I couldn't understand. "How could you not want to know?"

"Leave it, Aly."

"Was she expecting any friends to come over? Any classes that day—?"

"Leave it!"

The words "with Kyle" died in my throat. Anguish flooded my brother's face. Katrina died on a weekday. My brother had been at work, as usual. He used to work every day, all day. Maybe he felt guilty for not being there with her.

Before I could say anything to assuage him, though, he turned and walked away, leaving me with a mountain of old baby clothes and an equally large pile of unanswered questions.

~

Saturday morning was one of those random winter days upstate New York likes to throw out where the sun shines so brightly, you forget it's February. It was only forty degrees, but that felt like a tropical paradise compared to the rest of the month. Putting aside the weirdness from the night before, Kevin and I decided to celebrate the beautiful weather by going for a family outing. Even though there was still snow on the ground, with some fleece-lined boots and my thinsulate jacket, I'd be fine.

Shady Grove was primarily comprised of Main Street, filled with a handful of stores including Missing Pieces, and Second Street, which held a bunch of professional offices like Kevin's law firm and the town actuary/taxidermist. Beyond that we had City Hall and the bowling alley, which was currently for sale. Not a lot of places to go, even on an unseasonably warm winter's day. I assumed we'd head for Willow Falls, the next town over. It wasn't huge, but they had a mall and a trampoline park, both of which Shady Grove lacked.

Although we started out headed in that direction, we didn't go as far as I'd expected. For ten long minutes, my brother drove while Kyle and I peppered him with questions about our destination. Then, before I could beg for answers, Kevin turned into a parking lot and stopped. For a minute, I worried that he was going to tell me to be quiet or get out, but then he turned off the car and removed his seat belt.

"Here we are!"

Here? We were nowhere. I squinted to read a battered old sign at the edge of the lot. Branches obscured most of the text. "Maloney College Nature Preserve? Are we lost?"

Beside me, Kevin chuckled. "No, sister dear. The three of us are going for a walk in the woods."

"You must have me confused with someone else. I don't—"

"Walk! Trees!"

Whatever argument I'd planned to raise was moot now.

Kyle saw the dirt path leading into the woods, and he wanted to go for a walk. There was no way I could convince my three-year-old nephew that we'd turned in here by mistake after being cooped up inside for weeks. Still, I tried. "Want to go home and watch both Frozen movies? Olaf?"

"Walk!"

"Nice try," Kevin said.

"Seriously? We could freeze to death in there."

"It's forty-seven degrees. The snow is melting, and the path should be fine. Come on, the fresh air will do us good. Remember when we used to go hiking through the snow with Mom and Dad?"

"If I recall correctly, we were chopping down Christmas trees. You plan to celebrate St. Patrick's Day in style? Or are you looking for a Valentine's Day tree?"

His face went white, and immediately I regretted speaking without thinking. Katrina was born on Valentine's Day, so Kevin wouldn't be celebrating for a long, long time. He was getting better slowly, but we had a long way to go.

"I'm sorry, Kev. You know I didn't mean it."

He cleared his throat and pointed down the path. "You go ahead. I'll get Kyle."

Ha. As if I'd walk into the woods by myself. But I felt bad enough about what I'd said to stand and study the map at the head of the trail until the two of them joined me. My nephew took off excitedly down the path, leaving me with nothing to worry about other than keeping up with him.

The woods were oddly beautiful this time of year, even with no leaves. A stillness filled the air, one I didn't want to ruin by apologizing to my brother yet again. Instead I focused on keeping up with Kyle, pointing at things along the path and periodically responding to his steady stream of chatter, mostly directed at himself.

After a few minutes, our friendly conversation stopped

when Kyle came to a halt at a fork in the path about ten yards ahead of us. He pointed at a sign. "E."

I stopped beside him and read aloud. "Blue trail closed. Sorry, Buddy. We have to go this way."

He peered behind the sign, down the trail. "What's that?"

"That's a snow fox, I think." Suddenly, I felt uneasy. "I don't think they attack humans, but they might if they're protecting their food. We should go."

Kevin put one hand on my shoulder. "It's fine, Aly. They're harmless. One loud noise, and they'll take off."

To emphasize his point, he cupped his hands over his mouth and shouted, stomping his feet. The animals froze, looked up at us for a heartbeat, then scattered. I should've started breathing easier once the wild animals vanished back into the preserve, but something made the hair on the back of my neck stand up. Things just didn't look right.

"What's that on the ground?"

"Doggies dig!" Kyle said.

Kevin moved between Kyle and the animals. "Yes, the dogs were digging. That's what dogs do. Aly, why don't you take Kyle on down the trail? I'll make sure everything is okay and catch up with you in a few minutes."

A tremor in his voice told me he also felt something wrong about this place. We couldn't talk about it in front of Kyle, but I also didn't want to leave him alone.

I started to protest, but then I narrowed my eyes and realized what my brother had spotted before he rushed Kyle out of the line of sight.

A hand, poking up through the mound of dirt.

CHAPTER FIVE

MY HEART POUNDED in my throat. Nausea overwhelmed me. I couldn't breathe. The wild animals weren't sniffing the dirt. A dead body lay on the ground, barely covered by the snow, not fifteen feet from where I stood with my three-year-old nephew. This couldn't be real life. But it was.

Something terrible must have happened. People didn't just die while hiking through the forest and then bury themselves in the snow.

Snow. Sn. Sn was the symbol for tin. Periodic element fifty. Between indium and antimony.

Deep breaths.

"Kevin? Is that what I think it is?"

"Daddy, can I see?" Kyle asked.

"Sorry, no. This path is closed, right?," Kevin said. "The sign says."

"Sign says E."

"Yes, it does. Aunt Aly's going to take you back to the car."

Nope. No way. Before I moved to Shady Grove, the town hadn't had a murder in twenty years. This was the second since I'd arrived. I was starting to wonder if I was cursed. Or maybe people were just better at hiding deaths before I got here.

As much as I wanted to scream and run and pretend I'd never seen the person lying on the ground, I needed to get a better look. Which I couldn't do if I were taking my nephew back to the car. Kevin didn't know about my abilities, and I preferred to keep it that way. However, if I could get close enough to touch the body, I might be able to use my powers. Unfortunately, I couldn't touch anything with Kevin here, especially not in front of Kyle.

"Why don't you take him back to the car?" My phone was already in my hand. "I'll call for help and wait."

"I can't leave you alone in the woods. It may be unseasonably warm, but it still won't take you long to freeze. Come back to the car with me. I'll lead the police in when they arrive."

My mouth opened to argue, but then I snapped it shut. Kevin was a seasoned lawyer. He'd find it odd that the person who got nauseated when Kyle skinned his knees desperately wanted to hang out alone in the woods with a dead body in forty-degree weather. There was no good reason one of us needed to sit here and wait for the police. The animals had been scared off, and if they came back, I wasn't going to take them on.

Also, my phone didn't have a signal. Waving it in the air did no good. We couldn't call for help here. I followed the two of them back down the path and onto the main trail leading to the parking lot. We should get service there.

Halfway to the car, I stopped short. "I have to go to the bathroom."

Kyle glanced up at me. "Potty time!"

"Now?" Kevin asked.

"Daddy! I have to gooooooo."

I suppressed a smile. It would take Kevin at least five minutes to lead Kyle behind a tree and remove his snow pants while I slunk back into the woods, pretending to look for my own private spot.

Kevin sighed. "Go, Aly. I'll help Kyle and meet you in the parking lot."

"Sorry," I said without a shred of remorse.

Before he could respond, I turned and headed back the way we came. Alone, it didn't take nearly as long to navigate as when I helped shepherd a three-year-old. I made it back to the fork in the path in less than two minutes. Thankfully, the animals hadn't returned.

My footsteps slowed as I neared the body. While I needed to get closer to see what I could find out, the nausea that hit me upon first realizing what we'd found returned full force. The sight of blood grossed me out. I had trouble with dissections. In high school, I'd spent a week mourning once my advisor explained why it would be tough to achieve my dream of becoming a doctor. Examining a dead person was miles outside my comfort zone.

But it needed to be done, and fast, before anyone else showed up and shooed me away. Police hadn't liked it when I'd taken it upon myself to investigate Earl Parker's death a few weeks ago, and I didn't want to think about what Sheriff Matthews would say if he caught me bent over a dead body.

It probably started with, "You have the right to remain silent."

Okay, time to focus.

Having never analyzed a crime scene before, I wasn't entirely certain what to look for. A sign saying "It was that guy" would help. There were no footprints on the snow, but since the storm had come through last night, that only told me that this poor unfortunate soul had been dead and buried for at least six hours.

As I drew closer, a burst of icy wind bit at me. I drew my scarf up over my face. Then my foot crunched loudly on something. Oh, no. Ew. Please don't let it be bone. I couldn't handle stepping on a dead person.

Crouching down, I got as close as I dared. Something wasn't right. Pink and white fleshy bits covered the ground, but only where the dogs had been. They looked chewed. They also did not look human. One of the pieces looked suspiciously like a chicken wing.

Abruptly, I realized what happened. Whoever dug this grave had strewn meat around the body to entice the animals. Probably hoping nature would destroy the evidence before the trail opened up for spring and someone came this way. Their plan might have been successful if the temperature had stayed below freezing. After several months of cold that made our faces hurt, New Yorkers tended to head outside in droves at the first sign of warmth. To be honest, I was surprised we were the only ones here. We might not be for long—it was supposed to be close to fifty this afternoon before diving below freezing tomorrow.

No, I couldn't explain it. The weather here baffled me more than why anyone would bury someone in the nature preserve.

The grave was only a few feet long, suggesting the person inside wasn't terribly tall. It couldn't be deep, given the hand poking out. The body wasn't well hidden, barely concealed under a mound of dirt to the left of the path. In upstate New York, the ground froze early in the winter and stayed that way until at least mid-March. It couldn't be easy to dig a hole in frozen dirt, which is probably why the killer hadn't done much. Or maybe they didn't have a shovel. Hard to say. Most people carried snow shovels in their cars this time of year, but those were plastic. I sincerely doubted anyone could dig a grave with one. Especially in February.

Beyond the body, the path extended through the snow for about a hundred yards before turning left and disappearing through the trees. Having never been in this part of the preserve, I didn't know how far back it went. It looked like there was a wooden building off to the side, but there wasn't time to investigate. If I didn't return to the car soon, Kevin would tell Kyle to wait in the car and come looking for me.

Also, I didn't know which trail the killer used to get in here or where they went, but I absolutely wasn't going to consider doing anything that would leave my footprints as evidence on the other side of the body. Not when my boss had been arrested for murder just last month, and I was still standing here, probably leaving loose hairs all over the place. If there was evidence to be found north of where I stood, let someone else find it. My feet were staying planted firmly on the path.

Crouching beside the mound of snow, I took a deep breath to steady myself. The slow inhalation gave me one last chance to think about what I was doing before passing the point of no return. Sure, I'd helped solve one murder, but that didn't involve digging into a fresh grave with my bare hands or touching the body. The best thing to do was go back to Kevin, wait for police to arrive, and direct them back to the scene. I didn't need to be involved.

Still, something kept my eyes sweeping the area. The main trail the three of us had been following lay about fifteen feet behind me, not far. I paced back a few feet, eyes glued to the ground, but it turned out that with zero clue what to look for, I couldn't tell whether someone had been recently dragged across the path from that direction.

Thick brush and unbroken branches on both sides of the path suggested that any recent visitors to the site had been on the path, but alive or dead? Walking voluntarily or being forced by someone else? I didn't see any blood on the ground, but who knew what lay under the snow? Other than a body. I knew that.

As I thought about the grave, my gaze fell on the hand a second time, and my breath caught. Finally, I realized what kept me from going back to the car. Whoever lay within that grave had perfectly manicured fingernails, cut into blunt squares with lightning bolts on them. I'd seen those nails before. Spoken with their owner. Sat in her class only two days ago.

A sob escaped me. Unless I was completely off my game, I crouched beside the freshly dug grave of Professor Zimm.

CHAPTER SIX

MY MOLECULAR BIOLOGY and chemistry teacher was dead. The sweet, lively woman I'd first met at the university bookstore a few weeks ago. My soon-to-be advisor. The woman who taught my class less than forty-eight hours ago. The lunch I'd eaten before class hadn't even finished digesting yet. How could she be dead? Why would anyone want to kill a college professor?

The tightness in my chest made me gasp. I couldn't believe this. Didn't want to believe it.

B was for Boron. Bismuth. Bohrium. Beryllium.

As the familiar words went through my mind, my mind started to clear. Poor Professor Zimm. Who would do this?

I wanted to dig her up, touch her, see what happened, use my powers to find the face of her killer. But the temperature was barely above freezing. I had no way of digging, my brother and nephew were less than five hundred yards away, and police should be here any minute. I'd never manage to explain what I was doing before they slapped the handcuffs on me.

A tear trickled down my cheek, then another. I sniffled, trying to get myself under control.

Berkelium. Bromine. C was for carbon.

Averting my eyes helped a little. The sunlight glinted off the snow, temporarily blinding me. After I blinked away the glare, I spotted a dark object, standing out in stark contrast to the whiteness blanketing everything.

A button.

A lost button. Lost by whom? The button itself wasn't all the interesting, just a piece of round, black plastic with a raised edge and four holes in the middle. It was heavy, solid. Could've been dropped by anyone, at any time.

Except we were here, in February, with a layer of mostly unbroken frost on the ground and a shallow grave. That button hadn't been dropped by just anyone. It had to belong to either the victim or the killer.

Wait. The button! It could tell me something. Given that it lay on top of the snow, it probably hadn't come from Professor Zimm. The only other person who could have left it was the killer. And while I couldn't see who owned an item like Olive, I could see what happened while the owner was wearing it.

The button sat on the snow, tempting me. I should leave it. Tampering with a crime scene was illegal, and this must be one. Yet there must be hundreds of thousands of black buttons in the world. Police couldn't possibly trace this particular one back to the owner. Olive could.

I cursed the uselessness of my powers. If I could do what she could, I'd already know who the killer was and the entire internal debate would be pointless. This was why I needed to practice. In a few minutes, Kevin would come back to look for me. I needed to know what this button could tell me, fast. If only I didn't have to use it. I glared down at my zip-up parka. Not a buttonhole in sight.

Hmmm.

No buttonholes, but I did have thumbholes. They might

not work, but desperate times. I snatched the plastic off the snow before anyone could walk up and stop me.

Pulling my left hand inside my sleeve, I held the fabric open. With my right hand, I pressed the button through the hole intended for my thumb.

The grave vanished.

I stood alone in the clearing, shivering. Not from the cold. Shaking.

A hole grew in the ground at my feet. Not deep, but long. More of a trench, really. The blade of a shovel entered the ground, lifted dirt, moved it aside. Once. Again. The wooden handle dug into my palms.

Inside the hole lay a big lump, already mostly covered. Don't think about the lump.

Try as I might, I couldn't see anything about the person wearing the coat. No sense of height, weight, size, gender. The hands manipulating the shovel never came into view. I didn't even hear any heavy breathing.

Then I fluttered to the ground.

"Aly? Are you there?" A voice in the distance jarred me out of my vision.

The police had arrived. They couldn't see me yet, but as soon as they made a left turn, I'd pop into their line of sight. Before I could reason myself out of it, I stuffed the button into my pocket. Seconds later, someone crashed into sight at the fork in the path. No going back now. I'd take it to Olive to find the owner and then call in an anonymous tip or something.

Bonus: I could take it straight to Missing Pieces, and maybe Sam would be there, too. Always finding the bright side of murder, that was me.

Shady Grove's police force contained exactly two full-time employees, Sheriff Tim Matthews and his super-hot nephew Doug. His nephew who I'd learned recently was in a relationship with my best friend, Rusty. Doug wasn't happy that I'd nearly gotten his boyfriend killed a couple of weeks ago, so he might not be thrilled to find me at the scene of another murder. Especially one I planned to investigate, whether he liked it or not.

As expected, Doug moved into view first. He was a tall, lean Black man with a face that made him look barely old enough to drink. His nightstick and pepper spray—not to mention the muscles—made me feel a lot better about being alone in the woods at a murder scene, though. It didn't escape my notice that his coat had shiny black buttons like the one currently burning a hole in my pocket.

None appeared to be missing. Unless he'd lost one of those random buttons sewn inside as a spare. Not that I thought Doug would kill my professor. Just trying to be more observant.

Doug sighed when he got within normal speaking distance of me. "There you are. You're not messing with my crime scene, are you?"

My cheeks grew warm. "I was out for a walk with my family. Then I saw…." A lump rose in my throat. "I think it's Professor Zimm."

"You know her?" His eyes traveled to the body, then back to my face. "Whoever it is, they're covered. How could you recognize them?"

"Her fingernails. Professor Zimm teaches my molecular biology class on Tuesdays and Thursdays. Or she did." I swallowed. "I remember thinking her nails looked fun."

"Oh, Aly. I'm sorry." Doug's entire demeanor softened as he saw where I pointed. "I don't know a lot about fingernails, but those look pretty unique."

"Thanks."

"Look, we don't know who it is yet. Don't jump to any conclusions. Maybe the local salon was doing a lightning bolt special. It'll take time to identify what's going on here. Maybe it's not even a human. It could be a mannequin or…" When he realized that I didn't believe a word he was saying, he trailed off. "Are those chicken bones?"

"Yeah. There were some wild animals scavenging." I swallowed. "I think the killer left meat here to draw them in."

"Well, That's unsettling. But listen, Pete and I—" he gestured to the man behind him, who had paused several feet away to tap on his phone—"are waiting for backup. You should go."

"Pete?"

The man I'd barely noticed stepped forward, putting his phone away. He was stocky, with a salt-and-pepper goatee and wire-rimmed glasses. "I'm the medical examiner for Shady Grove and Willow Falls. Here to oversee the excavation."

Excavation. Medical examiner. Professor Zimm. My head swam.

"Aly?" Doug said softly. "Do you want me to walk you back to the car?"

I did, actually. I didn't want to be alone. But I also didn't want a police escort while I smuggled evidence out of a murder scene. Partially because I didn't know what Rusty told him about my powers, but also because I didn't want him to guess I was hiding something.

That raised the question of how I would turn in the button later, but one thing at a time. Maybe I could pretend it fell inside my boot and I didn't notice until I got home.

That would work if Doug lost his brain on the way back to the station.

"No, I'm okay. You stay here. Thanks."

I rushed down the trail before he could reply. Kyle and Kevin must be in the car by now. My brother would be mad if I didn't show up soon.

As I turned onto the main path, Doug appeared behind me. "Aly. Stop."

I froze at the steel in his voice.

"Tell me you didn't take any evidence from the crime scene." His voice changed to a pleading tone. "Just say it so I don't have to arrest you."

I didn't want to lie to Doug. I also didn't want to try to outrun him in a snowy forest. Instead, I dropped my hands to my sides. "How did you know?"

"Intuition. Guesswork. A bit of policing skills. Also, the snow held impressions that made me wonder and you stuffed something into your pocket when I walked up." He winked and tapped his temple a few times.

Wordlessly, I withdrew the button held it out.

"At least you're wearing gloves." He rubbed his face cheeks with both hands before pulling out a plastic bag. I dropped the button in. "Rusty trusts you. You helped us before. I don't know exactly what your deal is, but for his sake, I'm going to give you the benefit of the doubt. But this can't happen again."

"I promise," I said. "I'm sorry, Doug."

If only I could tell him the truth, that would make a big difference. But the truth would get me locked up, especially since I didn't have good enough control of my powers to give a demonstration. Olive's secret wasn't mine to tell. If she wanted to work for the police, solving crimes, she had decades to volunteer before I came along.

"I will accept your apology, barely," Doug said. "Listen, we need to talk. I've got some men coming to process the scene. Kevin and Kyle are waiting for you back in the parking lot. Do you want to come to the station later to give me a statement? Or should I drop by your house?"

"A statement? About the button?"

"No, about the crime scene. You found a body. We need to interview you for the police report. You and Kevin."

Right. Duh.

I didn't want to go to the police station later or have Doug come to our place. I wanted to stay close enough to the crime scene to have a useful vision. "Don't you need me to stay to make a positive ID?"

"Normally, we'd have a family member do that. You sure you know the victim?"

"If it's Professor Zimm, she teaches two of my classes. I spent over two hours listening to her lecture on Thursday afternoon. I'll recognize her."

"Thanks for the tip." He ran one hand over his short black hair. "I don't know what we're going to find in that grave or how long it'll take. No need for you to hang around."

"Okay, thanks." As I started down the trail, three men carrying a bunch of equipment marched past me. "Who are they?"

"Never mind that. Now go, get warm." Doug pointed the men toward the clearing before turning back to me. "Oh, and Aly?"

"Yeah?"

"I like you. You were a big help in solving the Parker murder, and you're Rusty's best friend. So don't take this the wrong way." I nodded, suddenly concerned for what was coming next. "If I ever catch you stealing evidence from one of my crime scenes again, I'll have you arrested."

My mind whirled in the car all the way home. Thankfully, Kyle insisted we listen to his favorite cartoon songs, so I didn't have to talk. Who would want to kill Professor Zimm? Why? What happened?

According to the giant map posted at the entrance, the Nature Preserve included five major intersecting paths, all with different entry points. There were several parking lots, including one that connected the preserve to Maloney's campus. With two dorms on either side of the lot and university buildings at the end, cars came and went all day, every day.

The killer could have come from anywhere, could have gone anywhere when they left. Or, for all I knew, they could still be in there. The preserve was massive. This time of year, with no one out for a hike, a person could hide for a while without anyone stumbling across them. Maybe in that shack I'd spotted. Or any one of a thousand other places. I needed to figure out how to get that button back.

CHAPTER SEVEN

BEFORE STARTING work the next morning, I headed down the alley to the local coffee shop, On What Grounds?. The owner, Julie, manned the cash register. My eyes skimmed past her and went to Rusty at the espresso machine, taking in his spiky black hair, round glasses, and muscular frame. When I first moved to town, Rusty asked me out, and we went to the movies. It was a nice enough evening, but I wound up believing that he wasn't remotely interested in me.

Fast forward a year: When Olive got accused of murder last month, Rusty was the one who helped me explore my powers so we could prove she was innocent. I'd enjoyed spending time with him. Then, while working undercover together, we'd kissed. It had been nice. And followed by absolutely zero reason to believe it had been anything other than an act. Especially after he'd told me he'd started dating Doug. Ah, well. They suited each other, and we were great as friends.

I watched the way he moved seamlessly from measuring grounds to steaming milk to pouring flawless cappuccinos, wondering if I would ever operate anything with that degree of confidence.

"Good morning, Aly." Julie's voice tore me away from those thoughts. As I stepped up to the counter, our eyes met, and she grinned at me, misinterpreting the way I watched her manager work. She also unfortunately thought Rusty and I were dating, because she'd witnessed that undercover kiss. "Large vanilla latte with extra foam?"

"Yes, please. And a medium americano." My heart fluttered at the reminder that I was about to see Sam again. It was love at first sight when we met a few weeks ago. For me, anyway. He hadn't seemed to notice me, other than as his mom's employee. In his defense, most of our time together thus far had been consumed with trying to figure out who framed Olive for murder. But I did it, so hopefully when he thought of me, he had positive associations.

As she rang me up, Julie said, "I heard the news. How are you doing? How's Kevin?"

Word traveled fast in a small town like Shady Grove.

"He's doing as well as can be expected," I said. "Luckily, Kyle didn't see anything. Or at least, he didn't know how to interpret whatever he saw."

"Thank goodness for small favors," Julie said.

Rusty caught my eyes across the espresso machine. "Do you need anything?"

"Other than to stop finding dead people?"

"Touché."

"Sorry." I gave him a wan smile. This wasn't the time to ask him to talk Doug into giving Olive a shot at that button. I couldn't even begin to imagine how that conversation might go. "I appreciate the offer, though."

"Well, you know…" He glanced at his boss as he handed over my drinks. "I owe you one."

"Don't be ridiculous."

"No, really. You inspired me."

"To never, ever go bowling again?" Our investigation-turned-fake-date at the bowling alley hadn't exactly gone as planned.

He snort-laughed, one lock of hair falling across his forehead. "Not exactly. Did you know I started working here in high school? Back when Julie's Great-Aunt owned the place. She called it A Hill of Beans."

"I didn't realize. No wonder you make such a mean latte."

"Well, don't get me wrong, I love coffee, but I never intended to stay here forever. My plans got stalled a bit last year. I've been cruising since then. Hanging out, working, living my life."

"Nothing wrong with that. It sounds relaxing."

"Maybe, but also, unmotivated. And unfulfilling." He paused. "After we investigated Uncle Earl's death, I realized, that's what I want to do. I've decided to become a private investigator."

"By the way, Aly," Julie called as she walked into the back room. "I hate you now."

"Rusty! That's amazing!" To Julie, I called, "Sorry not sorry."

She huffed, but her smile betrayed her true feelings. Despite not wanting to lose her manager, she was clearly thrilled for Rusty.

"So what does that mean? You're going to open your own business?"

"Well, yeah. In three years." He smiled sheepishly. "That's how much experience you need to get a license. But I can work for someone else while I learn the ropes. I've been applying at firms for the past couple of weeks. I'm starting with Investigations Unlimited in Saratoga on Monday."

"Congratulations!" Saratoga was about half an hour from Shady Grove. Not super close, but not as far as, say, New York City. "But how could you work at a place with such an un-catchy name?"

In Shady Grove, local ordinance required the cutesy pun-filled names for every business on Main Street to preserve the quirky nature of the town. A lot of stores within town limits followed suit, but Saratoga apparently didn't get the memo.

He stuck his tongue out at me. "My heart will go on, I'm sure."

With a glance at the doorway to make sure Julie hadn't returned, I lowered my voice. "What does Doug think about this?"

"He's thrilled. But also, he says if I get myself killed, he'll blame you."

That sounded like something Doug would say.

"Speaking of getting yourself killed—"

"Now there's an ominous segue if I ever heard one."

"Valid," I said. "Does Doug ever talk to you about his cases? Or, I don't know, leave paperwork lying around?"

"Just how terrible do you think he is at his job?"

"Sorry." Guiltily, I moved my gaze to the floor.

"Now that we've established that I am one hundred percent Team Doug and I would never tell you anything to jeopardize our relationship or an ongoing case…" He lowered his voice. "What do you want to know?"

"Did Professor Zimm die in the woods, or did the murderer take her to that spot after? I was thinking that if we knew where she was killed, I might be able to read some objects at the scene, get some information."

"Good point. Also, you found her pretty far from the main road," he said. "If they're looking for someone who can carry a body for half a mile, that dramatically reduces their suspect list. Professor Zimm may have been about average size, but she had to weigh over a hundred pounds."

"An excellent point." I beamed at him. "We're a good team."

"Not good enough, I'm afraid. I can't answer those questions." He turned back to the espresso machine and started foaming the milk.

"How thoroughly have you hiked the preserve?" Julie asked.

I jumped, not having noticed her re-entering the room. Really, if I wanted to play detective, I needed to have to work on my powers of observation. "Not at all. Just the one trail Kevin and I followed. Red, I think. And the body was on the Blue trail, which is closed."

"My great-aunt and I used to hike it all the time when I would visit her as a kid." She pulled out her phone and tapped a few times before turning the screen toward me. "Look. Some of those trails are pretty wide. Not the one you were on, but yellow and blue. A person with an SUV could drive most of the preserve."

The blue trail crossed the red one not far from where Kevin and I had been. Anyone who drove in wouldn't have to drag or carry a body nearly as far as I originally thought.

"What I can tell you," Rusty said, "is that rumor has it she was shot."

"Does that mean it was planned?" I asked.

"Not necessarily," Julie said. Sometimes I forgot she used to be a lawyer. "It just means that whoever did it had access to a gun. But the fact that she was buried in the middle of nowhere after being shot made it seem like this wasn't just a botched robbery. They went to a lot of effort to stop her from being found. Why?"

"Good question," Rusty said.

"Maybe someone knew they were with her?" I suggested.

My phone beeped with a text, interrupting our brainstorming. I jumped when the time flashed across the screen. "Listen, I am so excited for your new job, Rusty, but I've got to run to work. Sam's waiting for me to open."

"Go on, then." Rusty handed over my coffees, leaning forward to whisper. "Give Sam a big hug and kiss for me."

My face flamed. Rusty knew all about my crush on Sam, but Julie didn't for obvious reasons.

"I'll tell him you said hi. Oh, and Julie?" I hesitated, not sure how to finish that sentence.

"Don't worry," she said. "I won't tell anyone that you two are again butting into police matters that are none of your business."

"Thanks."

When I arrived at Missing Pieces, Sam sat behind the counter by the cash register, glaring at his laptop screen. The expression on his face was menacing enough to send even the most determined antique-seekers away.

"I hope you haven't been doing that long," I said. "You'll scare our customers."

When Sam saw me, his face transformed into a smile. "Hey, Aly."

"Hey. What's wrong? Is someone on the internet spouting fake science again?" Our mutual love of numbers and facts was one of the things that drew me to Sam. Well, that and the way his eyes crinkled at the corners when he smiled.

He shook his head. "I'm trying to get a jump on my moms' business taxes for the year. But their filing system— and I use that term loosely—is making me cross-eyed."

"Oh, man. I remember the time I tried to help with the numbers. Emphasis on tried. I don't envy you, my friend."

"Look at this."

I held my hands up. "Let me stop you right there. I brought you coffee."

"Thanks. Remind me to tell Mom to give you a raise."

It was on the tip of my tongue to tell him that if he wanted to thank me, he could take me to a movie. But I couldn't. For one thing, he lived three hours away. For another, if he knew I liked him, he might reject me, and then I'd have to stop thinking up names for our future children.

Marie. Grace. Christa. Albert. William.

With each birth, I'd remind my parents there were better ways to honor science than by saddling your children with names like Kelvin and Aluminum. If only they'd named me after the first woman to travel into space.

It occurred to me that I'd been dreamily staring at Sam for so long, he might start thinking about getting a restraining order. I cleared my throat and set both takeout cups on the counter. "I'll be right back. Just need to take my coat off."

As I hung my jacket next to Sam's black overcoat, I again thought of the button I'd found beside Professor Zimm's body. Did every male in New York wear the same overcoat? Closer examination told me this coat was slightly different, in that the buttons themselves were embossed with the manufacturer's logo. Fancy, but I also knew he got the coat here second-hand.

Since Sam hadn't been a suspect, that wasn't terribly helpful. But at least I knew if I stood two inches away from every man in Shady Grove or Willow Falls, I might know if their buttons could eliminate them as a suspect.

Let's call that Plan B. There had to be a better way.

Silently, I cursed myself for letting Doug see me pocket the button. Now that he'd taken it, I had nothing. Olive couldn't find the owner of an object I'd seen but since lost.

"Everything okay back there?" Sam called from the front.

Quickly, I returned to take my place behind the register. Sure, he was helping out, but I was the paid employee in charge of manning the store. Theoretically.

"Yeah, sorry. I was looking at your coat." He didn't know about my powers, and I was only about forty percent sure he knew about his mother's, so I just mentioned that I'd seen a button near Professor Zimm's body and wondered if there was a way to figure out where it came from.

"Did it have any distinguishing characteristics? A stamp on the back, a pattern?"

I shook my head. "I don't think so. Police took it for evidence."

"The good news is, that's their job. They know how to investigate."

Ouch. Unlike me, apparently.

I reminded myself that Sam didn't know I wanted to find out what happened, but he must've seen something on my face.

Leaning over, he squeezed my hand. A tiny thrill went through me. "I'm sorry. I know finding a body must be stressful. And I know how helpful you were when Mom got accused of killing Earl. I just meant—it's not your problem. You don't have to worry about it. Police will find the murderer."

"Thanks." I squeezed back, leaving my hand in his while sipping my coffee with the other hand. It felt natural, right even.

"You know, if you could get the button back from the police, Mom could tell you who it belongs to."

I choked on my coffee, sputtering a huge mouthful onto the front of Sam's light blue sweatshirt. Luckily, my beverage was going to kill me, so I didn't have to die of embarrassment.

Tears streamed down my cheeks. He patted my back helpfully while I tried to get control of myself. As soon as I could breathe, he unzipped his hoodie and slipped it off. Trying not to notice how well his grey t-shirt clung to his frame, I offered to go soak it in the bathroom sink.

He waved me off. "I'm sorry. I should've warned you."

"That might have been nice," I said. "You know?"

He chuckled. "Of course I know! She's my mother."

"I thought it was a big secret."

"Maybe to the rest of Shady Grove. But not to me," he said.

My cheeks grew warm. When he said it like that, it sounded hopelessly naive to think Olive had kept her powers hidden from the people closest to her. But—"She told me you had no idea."

"She worries that I would see her differently. She doesn't want to know. But come on. I worked in this store when I was in high school. Every summer during college." He paused. "You're not surprised to hear that she's psychic."

"No," I admitted. "I've known since the day I met her."

Not knowing what else to say, I didn't elaborate. I mean, okay, he was fine with Olive's powers, but he'd grown up with them. Also, she wasn't looking to date him. He might not want me around his stuff if he knew.

Oh no. What if I had visions of Sam with his ex-girlfriends when I touched something of his? What if we got close and I saw private memories? Bile rose in my throat at the thought. Somehow, I'd never considered those possibilities. Now I was terrified. Not just of Sam. Of dating anyone, ever again.

Maybe I could find a nice virgin. A guy with no history. Who had recently replaced all of his earthly possessions due to an unfortunate fire.

Sure. No problem. Our town of ten thousand people must be full of eligible men like that.

Too late, I realized Sam was watching my face as all these ridiculous thoughts went through my head. "You don't have to answer this if you don't want to, but, Aly… you're the only non-family member who's ever worked here."

I actually knew that. Rusty mentioned it when I started. He realized right off that there must be something different about me. Now I wondered how many other Shady Grove residents had noticed. Maybe my powers weren't as secret as I'd thought, either.

My brown eyes met his blue ones. His gaze was open, friendly. Not a trace of judgment. Part of me understood the importance of keeping my abilities out of the public eye, especially if I wanted to use them to find a killer. But at the same time, it was a small town. Rusty knew. Julie suspected. Olive knew. What harm could there be in telling Sam? Especially when I hoped to one day move things beyond an "employee and son of employer" relationship.

Oh, right. All the things I just said about having visions about ex-girlfriends. He could be wigged out, too. If he even wanted to date me.

"Your mom is a kind soul," I said truthfully. "I needed a job, and she helped me out."

"Uh-huh." His penetrating gaze made me want to be elsewhere, fast. After a long moment, he offered a shy smile. "It's okay. We barely know each other."

Huh? I must've missed something. "That's true."

If only my superpowers gave me the ability to summon customers, I could bring in someone else to distract Sam from this conversation. Alas, I had to make my own excuses. "I need to go check on the clothing racks. People like to switch tags."

"Okay, no problem." He gestured back at his screen. "I should get back to work, anyway."

I started toward the far corner of the store, but Sam's next words stopped me in my tracks.

"I know we just met, but I'd like to get to know you better. When that happens, I hope you'll trust me."

My head swiveled around as if of its own accord, and the rest of my body followed. Our eyes locked. My mouth went paper dry. He wanted to get to know me better. It was a bad idea for all the reasons I'd just thought of, but my brain and mouth weren't connected at the moment. "I'd like that a lot."

"Aly—"

A jingling bell behind me signaled the opening of the front door, cutting off whatever momentous thing Sam had been out to say.

I barely avoided screaming with frustration as I turned toward the newcomers with a smile. That's what I got for wishing I could summon customers.

CHAPTER EIGHT

IT WAS FOR THE BEST, really. Until I learned more about my powers and how to control them, I shouldn't be dating. Probably. I should ask Olive about that. But now that I'd thought about the possibility of kissing Sam and having a vision of him with another woman, I couldn't shake it.

How would I avoid that? I didn't know how to turn the visions off. I barely knew how to turn them on. My efforts to get objects to speak to me worked about thirty percent of the time.

The customer approached, and all thoughts of love and relationship went out of my head. After that first man came in, a flood followed. Yesterday's warmth had unexpectedly continued, and Main Street bustled with people desperate to enjoy the fresh air and sunlight. For the rest of my shift, I barely got time to breathe, much less ponder what Sam had been about to say. It was probably nothing, anyway.

Around three o'clock in the afternoon, I got a text that made all thoughts of Sam fly out of my head: Mary wanted to talk to me face to face! Yes! Not wanting to risk another missed connection, I wrote back immediately that I got off work at six and could drive to her. She replied, giving me the address and the most hope I'd had in ages.

Forty-five minutes after Missing Pieces closed for the day, I arrived in Willow Falls. Mary lived in a smallish colonial, with a cozy-looking covered front porch and gorgeous blue exterior. What would Kevin think if I asked him to paint our house? Before I could ponder that thought, a woman answered the door, stealing my breath and my ability to form coherent sentences.

It was like seeing Katrina again. They had the same honey-colored hair, the same wide brown eyes, the same heart-shaped lips I saw on Kyle's face every morning. Other than the fact that Mary stood at about my eye level whereas Katrina had towered over me, they could have been identical twins.

My mouth opened and closed soundlessly.

"I'm so sorry," she said. "I should have warned you there was a strong family resemblance."

I swallowed and blinked several times. "It's okay. I mean, I knew you were sisters, but I forgot you looked so much alike."

She took my hand and pulled me in for a hug, which felt oddly natural. "I stopped dying my hair after the funeral. It's much more noticeable now. Please, come in."

I followed her through the doorway into a large, open sitting room. She directed me to a chair and offered me some coffee from a china service sitting on the coffee table. Seriously, the best thing about this area was that quaint custom of serving tea or coffee from a gorgeous pot on a fancy tray. I swore it tasted better. Nice to see that the habit transcended the Shady Grove border and extended into Willow Falls.

"I'm sure you're wondering why I reached out to you, Aly," Mary said after we got settled. When I nodded, she continued, "My sister's death hit me hard. We were best friends, you know. Less than two years apart, and we did everything together. Played together, worked our first summer jobs together, even dated brothers at one point. When I graduated high school, I applied to the same college Katrina went to. She got me into her sorority."

"I'm so sorry for your loss," I said sincerely. Kevin and I hadn't been close growing up, but now that we'd gotten to know each other, I couldn't imagine my life without him. The pain of losing a sibling/best friend must be unbearable.

"Have there been any updates on the case at all? I check the news, but I never see anything. I called the police; they won't talk to me."

"I'm afraid I don't know any more than you do," I said. "Katrina was found in their home, exterior doors locked. Lying at the foot of the stairs. The only person around was Kyle."

"Ah, right. Your brother was conveniently away."

Her tone made my hackles rise. "Kev worked seventy hours a week to take care of Kyle and Katrina. There's nothing convenient about him being away, preparing to try a big case, when his wife was murdered."

She sighed. "My therapist told me not to bring it up. I should've known you wouldn't hear me out."

I stood. "Ms. Towne, if you're about to tell me that my brother killed your sister, then you're right. I'm not going to listen to that. He was choosing a jury in front of five hundred people that day. He didn't even leave the courtroom for lunch."

"And you're sure the time of death on the police report was correct?"

To be honest, I didn't know what the reported time of death was. I only knew what I'd found online. For this conversation, it didn't matter. "I know how much Kevin loved his wife. I see it on his face every day. He didn't kill her. I should go."

"Wait." She sighed. "I'm sorry. Please, don't go. It's so nice to see family."

Although I didn't want to hear another thing she had to say, a tiny voice inside me suggested that Mary might have something belonging to Katrina, and if she did, she could help me find out who the killer actually was, thus convincing her of my brother's innocence. Not that I could tell her that. But I could stay a bit longer. Crossing my arms, I turned.

"You're not the only one hurt by Katrina's death. Kevin gave up everything and moved to be near you, her closest relative. It must've broken his heart all over again when you accused him and cut off contact."

Her face turned red. "I was distraught."

"I get it." She probably wasn't going to give me a better opening, especially since I wanted to get out of here before I decked her for the things she was saying about my brother. "Did you have anything of hers? Pictures of her when she was a child, or anything? I'd love to show them to Kyle when he's older."

She nodded and moved to the bookcase, pulling out a well-worn leather album that probably started as red but had turned pink in areas. "Here. Family photos."

Yes! I settled on the couch next to her and reached for the book without hesitation. I'd never gotten a reading from a photo, but that didn't mean I couldn't. How hard could it be?

Very, it turned out. I examined photos, touched a couple, squinted, even closed my eyes a couple of times. Didn't see a thing other than the physical pictures. Page after page, I looked at images of two smiling, happy girls, often with their parents. The book covered from when Mary was about two years old until her high school graduation, hitting all the major milestones. By the time we got to the end, I didn't try to contain my tears, for her loss and Kevin's and Kyle's and the life Katrina would never know.

"Thank you so much." I blew my nose before continuing.

"I can't ask you to give me this album. It's too valuable. But could I make copies of some of the pictures?"

"Of course. Take it with you, and bring it back whenever you want." She hesitated, putting one finger to her lips. "There is one more thing."

"Yeah?" As much as I wanted to think we'd bonded over the past twenty minutes or so, I still didn't trust Mary. If she started hurling more accusations at Kevin, I was out.

"I have something belonging to Katrina. Something I hope you will give to Kyle for me."

"YES!" The word leaped out of me so forcefully, I wished I could take it back. Sounding overly eager was never a good thing.

She shot me a curious look. "It's just a token. An heirloom. Our family tree dates back to the Puritans, you know. I want our nephew to understand his heritage."

Inside, I danced around, punching the air and screaming with joy. An antique passed down through the ages to Katrina? This was exactly what I'd been hoping for! Finally, something that might lead me to her murderer. Answers were so close; I could taste them.

"Of course. I'm sorry. I've been looking for something of his mother's for so long, I'm just excited." Not knowing what else to say, I kept babbling. "When I have too much caffeine, I tend to yell out inappropriately, you know. People talk about it all the time. 'Aly's loud, she must have had too much caffeine again,' they say."

Shut up before she changes her mind, Aly.

"Right. Well, wait here."

It took all my restraint not to follow Mary out of the room to whatever it was she intended to show me. A family Bible? Family ring? A piece of Plymouth rock?

To my surprise, when she returned, Mary carried a perfectly Kyle-sized rocking horse. She set it on the floor and wobbled it back and forth. "I shouldn't admit this, but I took it from the house after Katrina's funeral. I know, I know… I was so upset, and I thought I should get it back to give to my children someday. Kyle would never miss it at his age, and I doubt Kevin remembered Katrina had it."

Since I'd never heard of a missing rocking horse, I couldn't comment on that. "Why are you giving it to me now?"

"Step nine. Make amends."

Ah. Kevin said she'd been in rehab. Now everything fell into place. She needed to return the rocking horse, even if she didn't believe that Kevin was innocent, because it belonged to Kyle.

I thanked her sincerely, promised to talk to Kevin about allowing her to see her nephew in the not-too-distant future, and hurried outside to test the horse. It took everything in me not to let out peals of joyous laughter. Something belonging to Katrina! Finally. She'd played on it as a child. She'd gifted it to her son. It was in the house when she died!

Behind my car, out of view of the house, I set the horse on the ground and gingerly rocked it back and forth. Nothing happened.

"Come on, come on," I muttered. "Please don't make me use a child's toy in public."

The horse was made of wood and it looked fairly sturdy, but it was meant to hold a forty-pound child, not an adult. The thing would crumple like an accordion under my weight. I had to do something, though.

Praying that no one was looking out their windows to see how ridiculous I must look, I straddled the horse and squatted. My bum hovered in the air about an inch above it. To avoid resting my weight on the old wood, I held onto my car doors for balance. *Please don't let this moment wind up on TikTok.*

I rocked forward a tiny bit, then lost my balance. It took every ounce of athletic ability I'd ever possessed, but I managed not to topple over. Still, this wasn't working. Okay, time for something else. This time I knelt on the pavement, one knee on either side of the horse and grasped the handles, like a child would. Smiling broadly, I rocked forward, then back.

Forward, then back.

The world fell away, as it did at the start of a vision.

Emptiness. A white wall. The buzz of nothingness.

With effort, I shook the vision away. I felt nothing. I saw nothing. I heard nothing.

Nothing at all.

Not a child's peal of laughter. Not the love of a parent watching their son or daughter using the rocking horse. Not the joyous glow of a grandparent passing the toy down to the next generation.

The horse didn't give me a single flash of anything. Despite, according to Mary, being hundreds of years old and having been in her family for generations. It was nothing but a blank slate, like a veil drawn over my vision.

How could that be?

CHAPTER NINE

THE NEXT MORNING, Sam covered for me at the store so I could attend the service for Professor Zimm. As much as I hated to ask him, Olive spent Mondays volunteering at the LGBT+ youth center in Albany, and I needed to go. He must have sensed something when we spoke, because he agreed immediately, no questions asked. Or maybe he could tell how important it was because I called instead of texting. Either way, sympathy filled Sam's voice when he assured me he'd be fine at the store for a few hours, and he'd see me whenever I made it. Told me to take the whole day off if necessary.

I didn't want to be here, to mingle with Professor Zimm's friends and family, to meet her husband. Funerals were weird and terrible. Sure, in my twenty-one years on this planet, I hadn't been to many, and the last one I attended was for my sister-in-law, so you could say I was biased.

But funerals were weird and terrible.

Still, I wanted to pay my respects. Her death made me sad, and being around other sad people might give me some comfort.

Also, okay, I was a total jerk because I needed information about who killed her. Wandering around upstate New

York in February looking for someone in an overcoat with black buttons wasn't going to help. I didn't even know if the coat belonged to a man or woman. I still didn't know if Professor Zimm was killed in the nature preserve or somewhere else, if she walked there or was driven. Was there one crime scene or two? One killer or twenty? Did she have any enemies?

To my surprise, the church was packed. There had to be at least two hundred people here, many of them not much older than me. I thought I saw her research assistant on the far side, and more than one face looked familiar from campus. She must've been a beloved professor. I sniffled at the thought. She deserved so much better than to get dumped in the nature preserve and covered with raw chicken.

Near the front of the church, a man who must be Professor Zimm's husband stood talking to the priest. He just had that look about him, the wretched despair of someone who lost their spouse. I knew it well—my brother wore the same expression for nearly nine months after Katrina died. He kept twisting the gold ring on his left hand as he spoke to people, as if it brought him comfort.

There was no way I'd approach Mr. Zimm to start a conversation now, and my phone told me the service would start in a few minutes, so I turned it off and slid into a seat at the end of the back row.

From here, I had a great view of the backs of the heads of everyone who'd ever attended Maloney College, most likely. Plus half the residents of Shady Grove. I spotted Thelma, the town gossip and former soap opera star, sobbing violently near the front of the church. Thelma loved nothing so much as being in the spotlight.

To my surprise, Tiffaneigh sat a few rows ahead of me, off to one side, between a guy and a girl I recognized from our class. Knowing my classmates also wanted to say goodbye made me smile. Brad hadn't put in an appearance, which wasn't surprising in the least. He didn't seem the sort to mourn a professor's passing.

Several people got up and spoke, telling stories loaded with inside jokes that meant nothing to me. I nodded along, chuckled where appropriate, and eyed everyone while looking for clues. This was where the ability to read auras might come in handy. No one seemed to be acting out of character for a funeral, but I didn't know any of these people well enough to judge. Except Thelma, whose one-hundred-percent in-character act told me nothing at all. This hadn't been a great idea.

The moment the service ended, she made a beeline for me. I should've known the town busybody would somehow know I'd been the one to find poor Professor Zimm. She had a sixth sense for gossip. "Aluminum! How are you holding up?"

Silently I cursed whoever gave my legal name to the *Globe*. "Please don't call me that. My name is Aly."

She sniffed. "Don't be ridiculous. Aluminum is a strong name, a noble name. Aluminum knows when to bend instead of break. Your parents are wise."

"Mom and Dad are hippie scientists. My name is Aly." Should've gotten a legal name change like Kelvin. "Anyway, I'm doing fine, Thelma. Did you know Professor Zimm well?"

"I thought you'd never ask!" Her eyes filled with tears as she clutched my arm with both hands. "I was so distraught to hear the news. We were like sisters! Known each other since the day I moved to Shady Grove all those years ago. Poor, poor Tammy."

Like sisters, indeed. My spine stiffened. "Her name was Tabby. Short for Tabitha."

"That's what I said, my dear. Maybe you should clean your ears." She blew her nose loudly, trumpeting into a handkerchief. Having seen her do this before, I wondered if it was her character's signature move on *As the Hospital Guides Our Lives*.

Wisely, I changed the subject. "Her husband looks so sad. I feel terrible for him."

"Oh, he's putting on a great show!"

I stifled a laugh. That was rich, coming from her. "What do you mean?"

"Mark my words, it's always the husband. He never loved poor Tammy the way she loved him."

If Thelma couldn't even remember her "soul sister's" first name, she probably didn't know much about Professor Zimm's relationship with her husband. Ignoring her comments, I asked, "Do you know if they had kids? He could probably use some help taking care of them."

"Yes, two kids, I believe. They're pretty young. He must've felt the service would be too much for them."

Seeing as how half the town had come to gawk, I suddenly felt a kinship with Mr. Zimm. "Yeah. Well, it was nice to see you, Thelma. I better go pay my respects."

"Wait!" She grabbed my arm. "You haven't told me a thing. Is it true she was shot in the back of the head, execution-style?"

With extreme effort, I avoided rolling my eyes at the insensitivity of the question. Not to mention the excited way she asked. Even if I knew anything more about my professor's death than what had been posted in the local papers, Thelma was the last person on earth I'd tell.

"I have no idea. I'll give your respects to Mr. Zimm."

It took half an hour to extract myself from Shady Grove's most dedicated gossip. She should work as a consultant for the police on interrogation techniques. By the time I joined the line of people paying their respects to Mr. Zimm, only three remained. Another five minutes, and I'd have missed him.

As it was, I wound up being the last person to step up. I

studied my professor's husband while I waited. He had short, mostly gray hair that thinned in the back. He wore thick, black glasses, but his eyes were so swollen, I could barely see the irises. Deep lines showed on almost every inch of his face, and I wondered how many of them had been there a week ago.

When I reached him, I gave only my first name, omitting the fact that I'd been the one to find his wife. If he remembered my name from the paper, so be it. "I'm so sorry for your loss. I'd only met Professor Zimm a few times, but I was excited to take her classes."

"Tabby loved to teach. She had such a brilliant mind. She could've done anything. I kept saying, if you put your mind to it, you could cure cancer." He sighed, shaking his head. "But she loved you kids. And now we'll never know what she could have accomplished."

"We loved her, too. Not just me. Look at how many former students came today. And she was great with my nephew when we met at the bookstore." Although I knew the answer, I asked, "Did you two have kids?"

He nodded. "Six and four. I thought this would all be too much for them. They're with my mother, who can't handle big crowds. She drove out from Boston to stay with us, to help out."

Mentally, I filed that information away. "I know you don't know me, but I've been taking care of my nephew for the past year. He's three. If you need someone to watch the kids for a bit, give you some time alone, I'm happy to help."

"Thank you." He paused. "What was your name again?"

"Aly. Why don't I give you my number?"

He nodded absently and pulled out his phone. He tapped on the screen. "I'll just text you. What is it?"

Although I rattled off the number twice, he couldn't quite seem to get it. From the faraway look in his eye, it was clear Mr. Zimm wasn't listening to me. He gazed at the picture of

Professor Zimm on the altar, the pain on his face so raw, I felt like an intruder.

"Why don't you give me your phone, and I'll input my number for you?" And, you know, if I conjured a vision telling me where he was when his wife died, cool.

He abruptly pulled himself together. "What? No. I'm sorry, I've got it." He read the number back to me, this time correct. At least I tried. My phone beeped with a text a moment later.

"Hold on. Aly?"

I nodded. "That's right."

"You're the one who found my wife's body."

I'd been hoping he wouldn't make that connection, but it was a pretty big ask of the universe, even considering how distraught he was. "I am. I'm so sorry."

"Don't be. At least she wasn't out there long." His voice cracked. "If you hadn't found her, it might have been weeks before someone else used that trail. My children and I would have been left wondering. Thank you."

"You're welcome" was one hundred percent the weirdest thing I could say here. Instead, I summoned my inner society lady from streaming old British TV shows. "I'm glad Kevin and I were in the right place at the right time. We wouldn't want your family to suffer any more than necessary."

"Tell me, did you see anything unusual at the crime scene?"

Other than the dead lady? Although I realized that Mr. Zimm must be distraught about the loss of his wife, his question rubbed me the wrong way. Almost like he was fishing for information.

"I'm sorry, but we left as soon as we realized what we'd found. We didn't want Kyle to see." Not entirely accurate, but true enough.

A long beat passed, then he nodded in understanding. "Of

course. Well, I'll let you know if I need a sitter. It was nice to meet you, Aly."

Right. My pretext for coming to talk to him, and my way into his house to find out what happened. "Great! Again, I'm sorry for your loss."

As I walked out of the church, I felt his intense gaze boring into my back. Something was not right with that guy. I'd bet money he was hiding something.

Thelma's words came back to ring in my ears. *It's always the husband.*

CHAPTER TEN

THE NEXT MORNING, I overslept for the first time in as long as I could remember. I blinked at the clock repeatedly when I woke up, as if not understanding the significance of seeing an "eight" as the first numeral when lying horizontally. After a second, I bolted upright and raced down the stairs.

"Kev? Kyle?"

The two Reynolds men waited in the kitchen, sharing a plate of toast. They both turned to stare at the doorway. My nephew's face lit up. "Aly!"

"Good morning!" I sagged with relief. "Kevin, is everything okay? Why didn't you wake me up?"

"It's been a stressful few days," Kevin said. "I figured you could sleep in for once. I'll take Kyle to school, and you can relax until your first class. I don't have any appointments until ten this morning."

"Are you sure? I can run up to shower..." As I spoke, my stomach growled.

"I'm sure. Eat."

"Aunt Aly?" Kyle looked up at me with his sweet face that always made me want to smile and tousle his curls. So I did.

"What's up, Buddy?"

"You sad. I don't want sad. I get you pwesent."

"Oh, sweetie, you didn't have to do that." Ignoring me, Kyle pushed back from the table and ran for the living room. I caught my brother's eye and whispered. "Where did he get me a present?"

"In his toy box," Kevin whispered out of the side of his mouth. "Go with it."

I smiled and smeared some Nutella on a piece of toast while waiting patiently for my nephew to bring me a couple of blocks or something. Mmmm. Heavenly. When Kyle returned, I wasn't disappointed.

"Here," Kyle said. "This is my lucky truck."

He handed me a tiny version of a bulldozer, a three-inch-long vehicle that fit into the palm of my hand. "Your lucky truck? Don't you need this?"

"No. Truck strong. Aly need truck."

My heart shifted at his words. It was an unbelievably thoughtful and touching gift from a three-year-old. Kevin would probably tell me Kyle didn't know what he was saying, but I preferred to think he did. I bestowed my brightest smile on my nephew, hoping he didn't see the tears prickling my eyelids. "Thank you, sweetie. I'll carry it around with me all day, and this will make me stronger."

"Dozer strong."

"Dozer strong."

We fist-bumped before he climbed back into his chair and devoted his attention to the plate in front of him. I slathered more Nutella on another slice of toast and munched it while pondering everything that had happened over the past few days.

A week ago, my entire focus had been on finding out what happened to my sister-in-law. Unfortunately, that got derailed not only by Professor Zimm's death but the fact that Katrina seemed to have been purged entirely from this house. Finding the key to the storage locker explained a lot—and it made me less annoyed at Kevin for getting rid of everything—but I hadn't had a single second to figure out how to sneak away and drive down there yet. Until I got a few days away from Shady Grove, the items in that storage unit might as well be on the moon.

Then Katrina's sister gave me a rocking horse that belonged to her. Perfect! Until I tried to get a reading.

I still had no idea why the rocking horse was blank. Objects either gave me a vision or not. Most didn't. This one was like looking at a vision that had been wiped clean. Was that even possible? Who would do that? How? And why?

The obvious answer was Mary, as the one with access to the rocking horse, unless the killer did it immediately after Katrina's death. Next time I went to town, I'd take it with me and see if Olive could tell me anything useful. For now, though, that was a dead end. I either needed to convince Mary to give me another family heirloom, or I needed to do more digging around our house.

It occurred to me as Kevin went to brush his teeth before leaving there was one room I hadn't checked yet. It probably seemed obvious that the place with the most memories of Katrina would be the master bedroom, but she never slept in this house. Also, in my defense, there was no reason to look until a few weeks ago, and I'd been kind of busy since then. Did I dare?

It took me approximately three-quarters of a second to determine that, yes, I dared. I mean, I wasn't going to try on Katrina's lingerie (if Kevin still had any), or roll around on her side of the bed. I just wanted to see if I could find a keepsake. Something that belonged to her.

Since Kyle had to be at school at eight-thirty, I gave him a hug and kiss goodbye before jumping in the shower. By the time I finished getting dressed, the house was empty. As soon as I verified they were absolutely gone, I made a beeline for Kevin's room.

The room clearly lacked a feminine touch, with black leather curtains covering the giant windows and a black walnut king-sized bed dominating the room. On either side of Kevin's monster headboard sat matching nightstands. I had no idea whether it looked like that before or if he'd replaced the bedroom set. The table that would've been Katrina's held only a lamp, whereas stuff littered the surface of Kevin's.

Crossing the room, I opened the nightstand drawer on Katrina's side. As expected, nothing but dust bunnies. Since Kevin moved here after his wife died, it wasn't worth checking the black walnut dresser that ran along one wall. He wouldn't have unpacked any of her clothes. Maybe a keepsake in his nightstand?

Having never lost a spouse, I didn't know what a person did to remember them. Or to try to forget.

Ow!

My toe slammed into the rear bedpost as I moved around the footboard. Oh, that smarted. My foot throbbed. This was what I got for invading my brother's privacy. Hopping on the other foot, I grabbed my left pinky toe as if that would somehow dull the pain.

Something clattered to the floor. What the....?

The truck. Kyle's toy truck fell out of my pocket. As I watched helplessly, it rolled away under the bed. Lovely.

Sure, I could leave it there. But I liked the idea of carrying something of Kyle's around with me at school, a toy to make me smile during a stressful day. Also, if Kevin found the truck under his bed after watching Kyle gift it to me, he'd know I was in his room. Not an option. Not after he told me to stop snooping around the basement.

I could almost hear him. *"That wasn't what I meant, Aly."*

Squatting beside the bed, I leaned forward and reached around. No dice. If I wanted to do this, I was going to have to risk getting dirty. Thankfully, Kevin had a cleaner come in every two weeks.

As soon as I lay flat on the floor, I spotted my prize. Reaching in, I let out an "aha!" when my fingers touched the cool metal. My triumph came too soon. The truck rolled away, deeper under the bed. Something rustled.

I gasped. If there was a mouse under this bed, I was moving back to California immediately. No, wait, the truck caused the rustling.

My fingers hit something stiff, smooth. Crinkly. Paper.

After retrieving my hand, I used the flashlight on my phone to peek under the bed to see where the truck had gone. To my surprise, I spotted a large, flat rectangle covered in brown butcher paper. A painting? A portrait of Katrina? Could I be that lucky?

The voice in my head had barely finished telling me to respect my brother's desire to keep this item hidden when I finished pulling it out from under the bed. This could be exactly what I needed to get answers.

As I dragged the heavy object out from under the bed, I recognized it. A large square, very similar to the one that used to hang over the side table in our living room. The item Kevin said he'd taken down a few weeks ago because the frame broke. A replacement or a lie?

I peeled the brown paper away, revealing an antique mirror with an ornate silver and black frame. An *unbroken* silver and black frame. Definitely the original. It even had a white mark on the side from when Kyle got a bit carried away with his new chalkboard wall and started drawing on every-thing. Why had my brother hidden the mirror? And why lie about it? Was it as simple as worrying that it would get broken? Or did looking at it remind him too much of Katrina because it was more her style than his?

My heart pounded. This was it. The thing I'd been waiting for. Much better than an antique toy, because this had been in the front hall when Katrina died. It might even have seen the face of her killer! With a description, I could call in an anonymous tip to police, breathing new life into the case. They could make a sketch, show it to the neighbors, and maybe find out the truth.

A huge smile splitting my face in two, I leaned over the mirror to see what it could tell me. A pale face with light brown eyes stared back at me. My chestnut brown hair swung down in wet brown ropes because I hadn't finished drying it before coming in here. I looked exhilarated, then immediately skeptical. That was it. No vision, just me. An image of myself was not helpful, since I already knew what I looked like.

Sometimes being psychic aggravated me. Why didn't my powers come with an instruction manual?

"What am I supposed to say? 'Mirror, mirror on the wall, who is the fairest of them all?'" My own reflection peered back at me, so either that wasn't the answer, or the mirror was feeling cheeky. By any objective measurement, Rusty was way fairer than me.

Not relevant at the moment, but true.

With a sigh of frustration, I sat back on my heels, glaring at the mirror. The clock on my phone told me I needed to leave in about twenty minutes. I made a snap decision: My hair could dry in the car. With a few quick taps, I opened a private browser window and started looking up ways to get the mirror to tell me its secrets.

The answer, apparently, was scrying. Some people didn't believe in scrying, but plenty of people also didn't believe in antique store owners who could sense the person an object belonged to, or a science major who got visions. Maybe my powers extended to scrying, maybe not, but I intended to find out.

According to *The Lone Mystic*, the first website to come up in response to my search, there were a ton of types of scrying, including using water, wax, smoke, or even staring into someone's eyes. Creepy. Other than Sam, I didn't have much interest in getting that close to anyone. Somehow, I didn't think Olive's son would let me gaze into his pupils for several minutes trying to read his soul, especially before our first date.

A lot of the articles seemed to think water scrying would be easiest for beginners, but since I wanted specifically to see what happened to Katrina, her mirror felt like the right medium. My eyes devoured the information until it was time to go.

We didn't have any candles or incense, both of which would help me focus my energy before attempting to scry. Our next-door neighbors, Mr. and Mrs. Patel, ran the local magic shop for their daughter Amira while she went on a spiritual tour of the world. She was wisely spending the next several months in South America before returning to warmer temperatures, but my neighbors would hopefully point me in the right direction.

Part of me wanted very badly to slip over to Mrs. Patel's house now, but there was no point. Rushing things wouldn't get me the answers, and even if it would, I doubted they kept scrying supplies at home. I'll Put a Spell On You was on Main Street, about fifteen feet from Missing Pieces. I could head over on my break tomorrow and get whatever I wanted. For now, I needed to go to class, see what I could learn about Professor Zimm's untimely death. Once again, my poor sister-in-law would have to wait.

With a sigh, I wrapped the brown paper around Katrina's mirror a second time and slid it back under Kevin's bed.

CHAPTER ELEVEN

IT FELT weird to show up on campus on Tuesday like nothing happened, but, for one thing, I had other courses and a strong desire to pass them all. Although Professor Zimm taught half my classes, my other professors appeared to be alive and well.

More importantly, showing up as usual and watching the other students might give me some important information. Since science majors had a lot of overlapping requirements, the same faces showed up several times throughout my day. Someone might know something. The more time I spent with the other students, the more likely they were to talk.

That guy with chin-length red hair might have information on who disliked Professor Zimm enough to kill her. Or maybe the guy sitting in front of Brad saw or heard something on Friday evening on his way back to the dorm. This was my best chance to talk to people before they started to forget or move on. I'd wanted to chat with Tiffaneigh and her friends immediately after yesterday's service, but then Hurricane Thelma hit, and by the time I'd extricated myself from her path, they'd left.

Unfortunately, when I got to Molecular Biology, she

wasn't there yet. Oh, how badly I wanted to dive into that seat in the middle of the front row. She'd be so annoyed. But I needed to investigate. It felt weird to walk up to total strangers and ask them what they knew, so I started with the most familiar face in the room.

"Hey, Brad." I slid into my seat from last Thursday. "Can you believe what happened to Professor Zimm?"

He narrowed his eyes at me. "What are you talking about? She didn't take a sabbatical, did she? Because if I have to take this class a third time, I swear I'm gonna blow a gasket."

"Uh, no, actually. I'm not sure how to say this." I took a deep breath. "She died. On Friday night. Someone killed her. You didn't know?"

His eyes grew wide. "Whoa. Seriously?"

I nodded.

Leaning forward, he poked the back of the guy in front of him, a Hispanic guy with close-cropped dark hair. He turned around, revealing a friendly smile and a chin dimple. Lucky. I always wanted dimples. "Yeah?"

"Did you hear Zimm bit it?"

With a shake of my head, I closed my eyes. Talking to Brad first had not been my best move.

The guy frowned at him. "Show some respect, man. A woman is dead. But yes, I did know. I went to her funeral yesterday. Why didn't you?"

To his credit, Brad's face turned red. He turned to me. "I was at a tourney in Rochester over the weekend. Took an extra day and got back late last night."

"It's okay," I said gently. "I understand you're surprised. But maybe consider how your words sound to others."

He thought about that for a minute before nodding. He slouched back into his seat, brow wrinkled, putting his feet up on the back of the desk in front of him. I was about to turn to the girl sitting on my other side when Brad shot upright again. "Hold on. Did you hear that if the teacher dies, we all automatically get an A? That would be killer for my GPA."

So much for that three seconds of introspection helping him grow as a person. My lip curled involuntarily. "Our professor is dead, murdered and buried in the nature preserve, and you're worried about your grade."

"Don't get me wrong. It blows that she died. But I've already taken this class once. I'm on academic probation. If I want to play during my senior year, I need better grades."

At least if the class got canceled, I wouldn't have to do a group project with this guy. I resisted the urge to bang my head against the desk. I needed to get away from him. Not knowing what else to do, I faked a sneeze into my elbow.

"Gesundheit!" Brad said.

"Thanks." I faked a second sneeze, then pushed back from the desk. "I'll just go get a tissue."

"No need." He dug around into the pocket of his coat and handed me a pack of facial tissue. "I always carry some this time of year."

"Thanks." I took one out, pretended to blow my nose, then offered the still mostly full tissues back.

He pulled something out of his coat, then fanned several additional packets. "Keep it. Look, I've got all these."

"You keep packets of tissues in your pockets to give out to people in need? Aren't you a good Samaritan?"

His face turned red. "Well, no. My dad told me it was a good way to start conversations with the female fans."

Of course he did. I started to roll my eyes, but then my eyes went to the arm of his coat. Heavy wool, as you'd expect in the middle of February. Big, shiny black buttons.

Black buttons with raised edges and four holes in the middle. Just like the one I found by Professor Zimm's body. Yes, it appeared to be a popular button. But Brad not only showed zero sorrow at the thought of a woman dying, his mind went immediately to ways her death could benefit him. He also resented her for failing him. Those things set him apart from everyone else. He'd claimed not to have heard, but was that true?

"Good morning, class!" A short, stocky man who reminded me of an older Jackie Chan spoke quickly as he strode into the room, forcing me to move my attention off Brad. Since I'd already been thinking about buttons, my gaze went immediately to this newcomer's coat. Camel wool, knee-length, so sparkling clean it might be brand-new. The buttons matched the fabric.

"My name is Professor Ng, and I'll be taking over for Professor Zimm. I'm sorry that I have to be here." He set his briefcase on the desk, revealing a thick bandage wrapped around one hand. Then he turned and leaned against the wood. "As some of you may know, Professor Zimm passed away tragically on Friday night. Her loss will be greatly felt by everyone on campus. We understand how upsetting this must be. If anyone wants to chat, I'll put the information for myself and the school counselors on the whiteboard. Meanwhile, this class will be canceled all week to give you time to process and grieve."

Tiffaneigh raised her hand. I hadn't seen her come in, but somehow this didn't surprise me. "Professor Ng? If we're okay, can we stay? I don't want to fall behind."

He did a double take. "Uh, no. Class has been canceled. You won't fall behind, because everyone has the week off."

"But I already did the reading."

"I'm sorry, what is your name?"

"Tiffaneigh. Tiffaneigh Pratt." When she spelled her name, I rolled my eyes.

"Right. Thanks, Tiffan-ay," he said. "Out of respect for Professor Zimm, we're all taking the week off from molecular biology. Before you ask, yes, her molecular chemistry class is also canceled. If anyone has an issue, contact me privately.

Next week. For now, class is dismissed. I'll stay for about ten minutes."

As everyone else filed out, I hung back to talk to Brad. If he was a murderer, this was a terrible idea. Then again, there wasn't much he could do to me in public in broad daylight. It's not like he knew I'd been at the crime scene.

As soon as he stood, I grabbed my stuff and followed him. "That's a nice coat."

"You like it? Thanks."

"Yeah, I was thinking about getting my brother one for his birthday." In August. "Do you like it?"

He shrugged. "A coat's a coat. It's warm, though. Fits pretty good."

"How are the buttons? Kevin's always complaining that the ones on his coat get loose and fall off easily."

Brad ran one hand through his hair. "To be honest, I've never thought about the buttons. They work, I guess. That's all I need."

"You've never lost one?"

"No?" His eyes narrowed as he looked at me, then he broke out in a wide smile. "You know, if you want to hang out, you don't need to make up questions about buttons. It's okay to admit you like me. That tissue trick works every time."

I stifled a groan. Here I thought my detective skills were improving, but clearly I still needed to work on my cover stories. "Really, I need a gift—"

"You're cute, Aly. I'm flattered. But I'm not looking for anything serious right now. Need to focus on the b-ball, you know?"

The only good thing about this conversation is that, as I avoided Brad's eyes, I was able to examine his coat. Every button appeared to be in place. Since I sincerely doubted he knew how to sew, he probably didn't own the one I'd found. The more I looked, it probably wasn't even that similar. Just me thinking I spotted a clue and getting excited. Without the actual button to compare, there was no way to know.

Forcing myself to put on a brave face, I looked back at Brad, who waited for an answer. "I understand. I hope we can still be friends."

"Sure thing. And hey, if you ever want to Netflix and chill, let me know."

I swallowed back the bile rising in my throat. "Thanks, but it's not my thing."

He shrugged. "Your loss."

Right. I'd super miss getting to spend more time with that ego. That's what I got for getting caught stealing the best evidence of who committed the crime. If only Doug hadn't taken that button, Olive could find the killer in about two seconds.

With Professor Zimm's classes canceled, I suddenly had a big block of time to kill before I had to be anywhere. Time to swing by the science building before physics. All the full-time professors kept offices there, and there was no place like someone's personal lair for finding items that might tell me about them.

Faculty offices were located on the second floor of the science building, on either side of a long hallway with multiple closed doors all in a row. As a biology major, most of my professors could be found here, which gave me a good cover in case anyone asked what I was doing.

To my great surprise (and relief), when I got to Professor Zimm's office, the knob turned easily. I'd been worried it would be locked, and to be honest, hadn't any idea what to do in that scenario. With a glance up and down the hall, I slipped inside, shutting the door quietly behind me and turning the lock on the knob.

The office smelled like a forest, probably because of the small trees scattered around everywhere. It looked like a perfectly normal faculty office, just like a dozen others I'd been in over the years. Instead of a traditional desk, a lab bench dominated the room. Behind it sat a raised bar stool that faced away from a computer monitor, as if the owner had just stepped away for a moment. Completing the illusion was the pair of glasses sitting on the table beside the mouse pad, as if she'd just slipped them off for a moment. A gray travel mug sat to the left of the keyboard, proclaiming "Without the Lab, You're Only Guessing" on the side. A lipstick stain along the rim reminding me of the bright red shade Professor Zimm wore both times I'd met her.

My vision blurred. Even though I'd hardly known her, this office was rife with personality. Anyone would have been sad to think about the occupant meeting with foul play. I had to remind myself that the best thing I could do for her now was to find the person responsible for her death. After wiping my eyes, I wandered around, looking for clues.

According to the syllabus, Professor Zimm held office hours on Friday evening. This should be one of the last places she went before she died, considering her body was found like a mile away. She couldn't have been killed here, though. Everything was pristine, practically gleaming. Nothing out of place.

Maybe her calendar could tell me something?

Sure, if this was 1950. Like the rest of the world, Professor Zimm probably kept her appointments on her phone. She did have a calendar: 365 Days of Cat Shaming. Frozen on February 6. A brown and black tabby cat wore a sign that said "I snuck in the closet and rustled around like a mouse the day after the exterminator left."

Hold on. February 6 was Saturday. Professor Zimm disappeared Friday night. Was she working in her office after midnight? That was a weird time to hold office hours. Or was she the type to rip off the page before she left for the day? If so, why only rip off Friday and not Saturday/Sunday, too. She presumably wouldn't be back until Monday.

Not knowing what to make of that, I took a picture with my phone but didn't touch it. Then I sat down at the computer to see if I could find out anything.

It was, of course, locked. The password wasn't anything I could think of: Tabitha, science, biology, Alb3rtE1nste!n... What a waste of time. She could have chosen anything from random letters and numbers to her favorite brand of toilet paper. I ran my hands under the keyboard tray just in case she'd left a well-placed sticky note, but no dice.

Unless my powers gave me a vision of Professor Zimm entering her password into the keyboard, I wasn't gaining access to her computer anytime soon. Sitting there with my hands poised over the keyboard got me nowhere, though. I did try, but no dice. Thanks for nothing, universe.

Footsteps sounded in the hall. With a glance at the opaque glass door, I stepped away from the computer and dropped to the ground. Hopefully whoever approached didn't also plan to break in and search for clues.

"You've made your decision?" A man's voice asked. His words carried clearly through the glass, and it only took me a second to get a mental image of Professor Ng. He sounded much happier than he did in class.

"Yes, absolutely. Congratulations, Gary. The paperwork will be on your desk on Monday."

Her voice sounded familiar. It only took me a moment to summon up a mental image of Dean Mendez, Head of the Science Department. She'd given a speech at Orientation last week.

"Be honest, Gabriella," he said. "Would I have gotten the job if Tabitha hadn't died?"

My ears perked up.

"You know I can't answer that," she said. "And it doesn't matter. Her research may have been compelling, but there is no one to carry it on."

"Well, thank you. I've been hoping to earn tenure for a long time. I'm glad I was finally able to prove myself."

Wait a minute. So Professor Zimm's death gave Professor Ng not only her course load, but also tenure? A lifetime job from which he could never be fired. Many people would find that to be the sort of thing worth killing for. An image of the bandage from his hand swam before my eyes. His coat wasn't missing a button, but it also looked brand new. Purchased since Friday night?

"There will be an official announcement next week," Dean Mendez said outside the door. "We'll talk later."

"Are you going in there?"

Metal scraped against metal. The doorknob above my head rattled, and my heart leaped into my throat.

CHAPTER TWELVE

MY EYES DARTED around the room furiously. In the small office, there weren't many areas to hide. Professor Zimm unfortunately appeared to have been partial to mini-pines, rather than the larger variety that would hide me (yet never fit in here). With a lab bench instead of a desk, there wasn't an enclave underneath.

"I have to water Tabitha's trees," Dean Mendez said. "If I can ever find the right key."

Taking that as my opening, I darted around the far side of the lab bench. I was still in plain view of anyone who came to stand in front of it, but at least I wouldn't be seen from the doorway. My pulse slowed approximately one-millionth of a beat per second.

"You don't have to do that yourself," Professor Ng said. His voice was softer now. "Can't you ask someone else?"

"I could, but Ethan called and asked me personally. I don't want anyone else nosing around in here, especially not before we find out what happened to her."

More scraping, a jingle, and the door opened a few inches, sending light slanting across the carpet.

"Are you even allowed in there? Isn't that a crime scene?" His voice rose higher with each word.

"I don't think so. There's no reason to think Tabitha died here. Police haven't said anything to me about it."

With the darkness when I'd first entered, I hadn't noticed anything on the floor, but now there was pretty clearly a dark stain. My fingers itched to touch it, to see what I could learn. If anything. But that would never happen. If the dean caught me crawling around the floor, I'd be lucky not to get expelled.

A phone beeped out in the hall. Dean Mendez sighed. "Not again."

"What's wrong?"

"The Pratt girl is harassing my assistant. She insists that she must be allowed to make up the classes we canceled."

"Kids today." Professor Ng snorted. "One of them asked me to change his grade from last semester 'under the circumstances.' Insisted Professor Zimm promised to do it on Friday morning."

"Sure she did." I could hear the eye roll in her voice.

Two sets of footsteps moved down the hall, and their voices trailed away. But I'd heard enough.

Brad told Professor Ng that Professor Zimm was about to change his grade. When we talked about it last Thursday, she'd adamantly refused. Now I wondered: did she agree on Friday and die before she got the chance to do it? Or did she get killed because she wouldn't make the change?

Before anyone else could come in, I dove for the stain on the carpet and put my fingers to it.

"Come on," I muttered.

I ran my hand across the fabric, trying to slow my breathing and focus. With effort, I shut out everything in the world around me, channeling all my energy into the stain beneath my fingertips.

A clatter. A thud. A travel mug hit the ground, popping the lid off. Dark liquid sloshed out, all over the ground.

A coffee stain.

I didn't know whether to be relieved that it wasn't blood. Professor Zimm could have spilled coffee at any time—my vision didn't come with a timestamp. From the flash I saw, the mug appeared to match the one currently sitting on her desk, but I didn't know if she had one travel mug or a hundred.

With a sigh, I pulled out my phone and snapped a picture of the stain. Probably nothing, but better to get the evidence now, in case I needed it. Maybe someone else could tell me if she always carried the same mug. I was officially grasping at straws. Or coffee stirrers.

A few minutes later, I snuck out of the science building, holding the door as it eased shut behind me. It wasn't until it clicked silently into place that I managed to breathe normally. Time to get out of here. Kyle was waiting for me—I'd promised we could build a pillow fort before bed.

I was halfway to the parking lot when I spotted Tiffaneigh entering the student center coffee shop. Without stopping to think, I changed course and followed her. Tiffaneigh had been pissed when she found out we were doing group projects, especially when she realized that Brad was going to be responsible for thirty-three percent of her grade. With only the project and one final, that gave him a lot of power to wreck things for her. Tiffaneigh was absolutely the kind of person who would do anything to get an A. Would she kill for it?

She'd also seemed way more concerned about her grade than a dead human being, although that appeared to be going around.

Given the way things went at our first project session, one hundred percent it would've been no surprise if Tiffaneigh had killed Brad. Maybe our professor was an easier target.

Probably not if she knew our classes would get canceled the following week, though. She missed two opportunities to learn. Possibly more: I'd heard that a couple of the other teachers canceled their lectures, too, so they could mourn.

With all these thoughts running through my head, I jumped into the line behind her. I made a show of pretending to study the menu board for a minute before I "noticed" her.

"Tiffaneigh?"

She spun around. "Oh, it's you."

"It's good to see you, too."

Her face softened. "Sorry. I've been on edge all weekend. The whole thing with Professor Zimm got to me."

"Yeah, it was terrible. I've walked that trail, you know? It could've been me." I declined to mention that I'd been the one to find and initially identify the body.

She shuddered. "I've been having nightmares all week."

"Me, too—"

"We might have to take the class over!" My sympathy for Tiffaneigh was quickly evaporating. "How could anyone do this to us? All the other classes are full, and now I might have to take summer school to stay on track for early graduation!"

"Yeah," I said slowly. "That's the worst part of someone murdering our professor. Not the fact that she was a human being with kids and a family who will miss her. Not that her life ended too quickly. Our grades."

I spun around and started for the door. I'd never wanted coffee in the first place, and the thought of continuing to listen to Tiffaneigh's narcissistic rants made my stomach hurt. After about three steps, though, she stopped me.

"Aly, wait. I'm sorry." I tilted my head and waited, but didn't say anything. "You must think I'm a terrible person."

"I hate to say it, but you're doing a pretty good impression of one."

"Don't go. Let me buy you a coffee, and we'll chat."

If she wanted to talk about the project, I'd drop my vanilla latte in her lap. But she seemed sincere, and if I got close enough to put my hands on something that belonged to her, I might find out whether she did it.

We waited quietly until it was time to place our orders. Partially because I couldn't think of anything else to say and partially because I needed to figure out how to provoke a vision. Not all items carried impressions. Other than the coffee stain, every vision I'd had involved either an item of great importance to the owner or an extremely important event, like a death. The coffee stain may have been brought on by my extreme stress, or possibly that of Professor Zimm. I'd have to ask. Would Tiffaneigh's backpack carry any impressions? She was certainly a devoted—if obsessive —student.

Once we had our drinks, I made my way to a table with three chairs and dropped into one, setting my backpack on the seat beside me. To my great delight, Tiffaneigh set her bag on top of mine. Excellent. Now I just needed to distract her enough to "accidentally" walk out with the wrong bag.

She cradled her cup in her hands, staring at the surface for so long, I wondered if she saw fortunes in the patterns on the foam. I was about to ask when she met my eyes. "I get it. You're trying to find out who killed Professor Zimm."

I swallowed, hating that she found me so transparent. "That's ridiculous. Why would I do that?"

She shrugged. "I don't know, but it makes sense. You were talking to Brad after class, then you went into the science building. You followed me into the coffee shop to question me. Plus, you know, it's only natural for the person who found the body to be curious about what happened."

My mouth fell open. Maybe she was psychic, too. "How did you know?"

"My dad's a cop. He told me one of my professors was killed and a girl in my class found the body."

"It could've been anyone."

"True, but when I said 'poor girl,' he said, 'That's not the worst part. Her parents named her Aluminum.'"

My cheeks burned. "I was born on the thirteenth. It's the thirteenth element."

She laughed. "Good thing you weren't born two days earlier, huh, Sodium?"

Heh. It was an obvious joke, but only because I made it all the time. The fact that Tiffaneigh parroted one of my favorite quips made me like her much better.

"At least I like Aly." A long sip of latte steadied my nerves. It was hot, burning a little as it went down my throat, but I relished the familiar sensation. "So, your dad's a cop?"

"Yeah. So before you go thinking I had anything to do with Professor Zimm's death, realize that I would've hidden the body much better than dropping it on a path and waiting for snow."

"This conversation got dark fast."

"Look, let me give you some advice," she said. "Drop it."

"Why? Don't you want to know what happened?"

"Sure, but leave it the professionals. You don't know what you're doing. If the wrong person finds out you're hunting a killer, you could get hurt."

Didn't I know it. I debated mentioning that I'd helped solve a murder only a few weeks ago, before realizing the difficulty in explaining how I'd done it. If the average person didn't believe in psychics, the average science major would start avoiding me for even suggesting the possibility they might exist.

A week ago, I'd have wanted Tiffaneigh to avoid me. Now, I wasn't so sure. Her attitude still chafed, but she had a lot more going on under the surface than what she showed the world. I got that.

"I'm being careful," I said finally.

Her phone buzzed, and she pulled it out, tapping away. "OMG."

"What's wrong?"

"Professor Ng wants to cancel our group project! No. No, way! I've already done all the work."

I fought the urge to roll my eyes. Why would anyone ever complain about not having to do a group project? "*All* the work? We're supposed to track the growth over several weeks."

"Come on. I looked up what's going to happen. I just need to go back to Brad's house every week or so to take pictures."

I started to point out that Brad lived in his house and seemed perfectly capable of sending us pictures when I realized it didn't matter anymore. "Sorry you'll miss that."

"Oh no, you don't!" She tapped away on the screen. "Hold on, I have to fix this."

"It's fine."

"No no no no."

She wasn't talking to me. She wasn't paying any attention to me anymore. I might not have been there. It was now or never. Tiffaneigh was so absorbed in her phone, she wouldn't notice me walking away with her backpack.

"Thanks for the coffee," I said. "I've got to go."

Pretending to be in a hurry, I jumped up, grabbed her bag off the chair, and swung it onto my back. Trying to trigger a vision sometimes created incredibly awkward moments. Like now. But I had to know. Screwing my eyes shut, I forced myself to think hard about last Friday night. I didn't know if it would work, but the last thing I needed was to see the time she showed up for a final less than twenty minutes early.

Tiffaneigh vanished. I sat at a very familiar-looking table. Two coffee mugs and a slew of papers covered the surface in front of me. I looked up, startled to find myself meeting Brad's eyes.

"Thanks for helping me out with this," he said. "I need an A."

"Yeah, well, I need your five hundred bucks," I said. "Lucky for you, I had some free time tonight."

"Yeah, lucky me."

A grandfather clock chimed. With a start, I realized I was sitting in Brad's house. Tiffaneigh left with me on Thursday. When did she go back?

"When's your mom coming home?" I asked suddenly.

"Couple hours. Why?"

I ignored the question. "Why don't you show me your bedroom?"

"You serious? I ask you for one tutoring lesson and you want to go steady?" His hollow laugh made me want to smack him, but didn't seem to bother Tiffaneigh in the slightest.

"Get over yourself," she said. "This is just something to do on a Friday night."

A gasp escaped me. Oh, man, did I not want to know the thing I knew now. Tiffaneigh and Brad? Why? She'd seemed to hate him when we were working together. And Brad! He'd hit on me less than an hour ago.

I dropped the bag, bringing the coffee shop slowly back into view. My skin still tingled from the vision.

Tiffaneigh peered up at me from her spot on the table. "Are you okay?"

"Yeah, sorry." I struggled upright before placing her bag at her feet. "I grabbed your backpack by mistake, and the unexpected weight made me slip."

"You've got to pay more attention to your surroundings," she said, "especially if you're going to catch a murderer. That's one thing my dad always taught me. Constant vigilance."

"Thanks for the tip. I'll see you later."

After that vision, I couldn't leave the coffee shop fast enough. But at least I knew Tiffaneigh wasn't a killer. She wasn't anywhere near the nature preserve at the time of Professor Zimm's death.

CHAPTER THIRTEEN

ONCE I GOT HOME, I spent the whole evening trying to get a vision from that stupid wooden horse. I wanted to learn to scry, but the weirdness of the horse made cracking it a priority. It felt like looking at it through the back of a one-way mirror. I could see it, but my powers slid right over the surface. The internet wasn't much help, but it's not like I'd been doing this long enough to know where to look. By the time I went to bed on Tuesday night, I was exhausted and frustrated.

Something was off. And when things were off with my powers, I went straight to Missing Pieces. Although the store didn't open until nine, Olive usually showed up early to get ready for the day. As soon as I dropped Kyle off at preschool, I raced over, not even stopping for my morning latte.

"Is Sam here?" The words were out of my mouth practically before I'd crossed the threshold. Only after I asked did I realize that, if Sam was in the store, I didn't have a good excuse for asking about him.

A look of surprise crossed Olive's face. Possibly because I was carrying a rocking horse. "No, he's at the gym. You brought him a rocking horse?"

"Okay, good. And no, I brought you a rocking horse." I stopped to gather my thoughts. In my excitement, my mind was racing all over the place.

"Aly? You're almost an hour early. Is everything okay?"

"Honestly, I'm not sure." I set the toy on the bistro table near the register. "I met Katrina's sister yesterday, and she gave me this rocking horse that belonged to the family for generations. I'm desperate to see what it can tell me. You. Us."

"That's wonderful!" Olive clapped her hands together. "Did you have a vision? Actually, I suppose you would have opened with that… So that's why you were asking if Sam was here. What happened?"

"I tried."

"I'm guessing it didn't work. My powers wouldn't be needed if you'd seen Katrina's death."

Instead of confirming her guess, I asked, "Is it possible to have a cold in my powers? It was weird."

"Weird how?"

"My vision was blank. Like, I saw and felt nothing. A vision of blankness. Is that a thing?"

"If you had it, it must be a thing," she said. "But the question is, why would that happen?"

"Am I being blocked? According to Mary, the rocking horse was in the house when Katrina died. She owned it, and that was an important event." I sighed. "I thought I would see her death. This is so annoying. Even if the killer's face wasn't there, I should have gotten something."

Olive tsked. "I understand that. You must be disappointed."

"I am, but there's more. With a family heirloom, something that's been passed down for generations, you'd expect to get something off it. Even if it wasn't an item that had meaning to Katrina herself, a parent? A grandparent? No one in the entire Towne line cared about this thing at all, yet they keep on passing it to their kids? I don't buy it." I sighed heavily as I reached out and pushed on the nose, letting it rock back and forth. "Anyway, I thought you could confirm if it really belonged to the Townes. Maybe Mary was messing with me. Or maybe she wanted a gift for Kyle, and she thought I'd be more likely to give it to him if she produced something meaningful."

"Why go to all that trouble?" Olive asked. "Couldn't she just show up and give Kyle a present?"

I shrugged. "She thinks Kevin killed her sister. For all I know, this rocking horse is a nanny cam, and she just wants to get a view inside our house."

She let out a chuckle. "In that case, she'd probably use something easier to plant a camera in. It would take about thirty seconds to search this for a bug."

"A tiny bug?" I sighed. "Fine. I'm worried if I put my full weight on the horse and rock, I'll break it. But I did everything else. Even straddled and hovered, which had to look ridiculous. It wouldn't give me anything."

Olive came around the counter and peered at the horse. She examined it carefully, walking in a circle around the table. She scrutinized the faded pinkish saddle, the matching bridle, the features of its face. After a long moment, Olive reached out and touched the wood.

She screamed.

CHAPTER FOURTEEN

MY BLOOD CURDLED. "Olive? What's wrong?"

Instead of answering, she shuddered. Her eyes rolled back in her head. Racing forward, I yanked her hand off that rocking horse, desperate to break the connection.

"Are you okay?"

She didn't answer. She fainted.

"Olive!" With a speed I didn't know I could manage, I dropped her hand and leaped forward, barely catching her before she hit the ground. "Help! Maria? Sam? Anyone?"

The store was deserted at this hour, but if I got lucky, maybe Olive's wife wouldn't have left for work yet. Still holding Olive upright, I glanced at the clock on the wall. It was even earlier than I thought. Screaming would only help if people happened to be close enough to hear. Given our distance from the door and the thickness of these old walls, I didn't love my odds.

Carefully, I lowered Olive to the floor. My first instinct should have been to call 911, but what would I tell them? She'd been attacked psychically by a child's rocking horse? She was breathing, her pulse felt regular. Just...she'd fallen unconscious for no medical reason.

After a moment's consideration, I called the coffee shop next door.

"On What Grounds?, this is Rusty. How can I help you?"

"Oh, thank goodness you're there. Can you come over? I need your help." When I'd first discovered my powers, Rusty had helped me experiment. He'd been with me when I solved the murder Olive had been accused of committing. Now, when I told him she'd passed out, he hung up on me.

The thing with knowing you can count on someone is, you don't even worry when they appear to be abandoning you. Instead of getting upset, I sat on the floor, cradling Olive's head in my lap while I waited.

Less than thirty seconds later, the back door flew open. Rusty still wore his green apron and name tag. He must've dashed across the alley connecting our stores. When he saw us, he raced across the room and fell to his knees. I remained quiet while he checked her vitals, just like me. He apparently reached the same conclusion I did: that we weren't doctors.

"A rocking horse did this?"

"Sort of. She was trying to find out who the owner was." As close as we'd become, Rusty didn't know the details about my sister-in-law yet, and for some reason, I felt weird sharing her death with him. It felt more private than the other things we'd been through.

Or maybe I just hated to admit I kept hitting a wall. Sometimes I worried that Katrina's killer would never be found. Nothing I did brought me any closer to the truth, and now I'd injured Olive in the process. Maybe it was a sign to give up. Also, this wasn't the time.

"So what's up with the horse? Is it possessed?"

Having Rusty by my side relaxed me until I no longer felt like panicking. I was worried, but we'd figure this out. "No idea. It's weird. It's an antique, so I should have gotten a vision. Some prior owner, somewhere. But I guess no one had a strong attachment to it. I don't know. Maybe my powers don't work on toys."

He opened his mouth but must've changed his mind about whatever he wanted to say and closed it. He put one hand under Olive's nose, apparently checking her breathing.

"Should we move her? On medical shows, they always say not to move someone who may have severed their spine."

"I don't think her spine is severed. She fainted. I caught her and laid her on the ground. She didn't hit anything."

"Okay, good." Rusty adjusted his stance, crouching on the ground as he slid one hand under Olive's knees and the other behind her back. "Is there a couch in here?"

"Yeah, there are a couple in the back corner with the other antique furniture. By the armoires." Suddenly I was reminded that we were in a very public place with an unconscious store owner. The front doors were locked, and the sign said Closed, but anyone could look inside the windows and see us. "Let's take her upstairs. More privacy."

"Good thinking." Rusty nodded toward the rear exit. "After you."

"Do you need help with her?"

"Nah. I should be fine. Just get the doors."

I led Rusty through the back of the shop, past the hallway containing a small restroom and the outside entrance, to the stairs that led to Olive and Maria's apartment. Then I stopped, frowning.

"What's wrong?"

"I don't have a key."

Rusty moved past me and started up the stairs. "So? This is Shady Grove."

He had a point. Few people ever bothered to lock their doors around here, and Olive worked less than five hundred feet away from her home. She went back to her apartment at least once a day to get something.

When we reached the top of the stairs, Rusty stood back

on the landing while I reached for the knob. Sure enough, the door swung open.

Having never been in Olive's apartment, this felt like an invasion of her privacy. I hovered on the threshold, both wanting to look inside and feeling like I shouldn't. But Rusty couldn't hold Olive forever, and we needed to figure out how to help her, so I took a deep breath and stepped over the threshhold.

For some reason, I'd expected my boss's home to look like the store—stuffed to the brim with fabulous antiques in a way that made the cluttered shop seem empty. Instead, a modern, pristine apartment met us. Rusty moved past me into the living room that closely resembled the front page of a Pottery Barn catalog. He didn't ask where the bedroom was, probably feeling like me, that it would be too much of an intrusion. Instead, he laid Olive gently, almost reverently, on the couch, using a pillow to cushion her head. I removed her shoes and picked up a plush throw to cover her. Her chest still rose and fell, but her face remained the color of homemade play dough.

"One of us should get Maria," Rusty said, breaking into my thoughts. "Do you want to go or should I?"

If Maria was teaching a class, she wouldn't answer the phone, but she needed to know what happened. It made more sense for me to go, since Rusty didn't see Olive's collapse. Yet, I didn't want to leave my boss, even with Rusty to watch over her. I wanted to stay and hold her hand and make sure everything would be okay.

Later. Now, I needed to be strong. Olive would be fine. Psychic injuries weren't fatal, were they? It occurred to me that I didn't know, and I started to worry again. What if the horse attacked her brain? What if she never woke up? What if she couldn't talk or remember any of us? What if—

Rusty reached out and touched my arm. "Hey. Look at me."

Wordlessly, I obeyed.

"Look at me. Concentrate on my face." I could do that. "You're panicking. Whatever you're thinking, stop. Take a deep breath."

He breathed in and out with me for a minute, counting slowly. Then he said, "Getting upset won't help Olive. Right now, she's our number one focus."

"You're right, I'm sorry."

"Don't apologize. Just stay with me. Do you want me to find Maria?"

"No, I'll go." My lips trembled at the words. I wanted to be strong. We needed to tell Olive's family. I didn't want to call Sam until we found Maria, and he'd be back soon. I could do this.

Unfortunately, my bravado didn't make it out the door. I took exactly two steps toward the stairway, then burst into tears.

"Oh, Aly. I'm sorry." Before I could move, Rusty's arms encircled me. I wept into his shoulder, letting loose all of my fears. He stroked my hair, murmuring soothing sounds that I didn't even understand. It didn't matter. They did their job, permeating my brain and helping me feel less stressed.

Or maybe that was the smell of coffee on his clothes. I felt more at peace with every breath I took.

After what felt like forever, I took a long breath.

"Thank you," I mumbled into his shoulder.

"No problem. Whatever you need, I'm here for you."

Footsteps on the stairs alerted me to the fact that we hadn't closed the door behind us. I started to pull away, but whoever was there made it up to the landing in seconds.

Sam's voice rang out from the doorway. "Mom? What happened?"

I spun around as his eyes landed on me and Rusty.

"What are you two doing in our apartment?"

CHAPTER FIFTEEN

OH, no. This was absolutely not what I needed. Sure, Sam had never shown any romantic interest in me, despite my hopes. Still, the last thing I needed was for him to think I was involved with someone else. Especially not my gay best friend.

"Sam!" I pulled away from Rusty and pasted a smile on my face. "I'm so glad you're here. I was just about to go get Maria."

"What happened?" Sam asked again. Not waiting for a reply, he rushed past me to the couch and dropped to his knees. "Mom? Mom! Wake up! Have you guys called 911? Why didn't you call me?"

No, no we had not and all of a sudden I didn't have a reasonable explanation. Paramedics presumably couldn't help with mystical problems. I'd be more likely to get useful assistance from Mr. Patel at I'll Put a Spell on You. None of which I could tell Sam.

"We were just about to do that," Rusty said. "We wanted to make her comfortable first."

"She fainted," I said. "How did you know she was hurt?"

"I didn't. I finished my workout and came back to shower," Sam said. "Did she have a heart attack? A stroke? How could you move her? You might have severed her spine!"

I resisted the urge to roll my eyes. "She didn't fall or hurt her back. She fainted."

"Thanks, Dr. Reynolds," Sam said. "I'll take care of her from here. You two should…just go."

A wave of shame hit me. The only thing worse than Sam thinking I was involved with someone else was him thinking I cared so little for his mother that I'd get caught up in a romantic moment while she might be dying.

None of us knew what happened to her. Yet there I was, failing to get her medical attention. If I wasn't going to call an ambulance right away, I should've called Maria or Sam first. The longer I thought about it, the less it made sense to bring Rusty into this, especially from Sam's perspective.

"It's not what you think," I said. "I was upset after watching your mom collapse. Rusty was comforting me. We were about to go get help."

Behind us, Olive moaned. Relief rushed through me. All three of us turned, just as her eyes fluttered open. She looked from me to Sam to Rusty and back again.

"Why do I feel like Dorothy at the end of *The Wizard of Oz*?"

"Are you okay?" I asked.

"Mom, what happened?" Sam said at the same time.

She thought for a minute. "I think I'm okay. I've got one heck of a headache, but otherwise, I'm fine."

"We should go to the hospital," Sam said. "Can you move?"

"No, no, that won't be necessary," she said. "I overexerted myself. Forgot to eat today."

Rusty and I exchanged a look. Olive insisted Sam didn't know about her powers, and I hadn't yet found a way to explain that she was wrong. I also wasn't sure if she knew Rusty figured it out a couple of years ago.

"If you're okay, I should go open the store," I said. "Olive, please text me when you're up to talking."

She smiled a wry smile. "Or I'll call, like an old person. You better answer."

Rusty took a few steps away from me, then paused. "I should get back to the coffee shop. Julie will be wondering what happened to me. I answered the phone, dropped it, and raced out."

"Thanks for your help," I said.

"No problem." At the door, he paused and looked back over his shoulder. "Oh and Sam? Aly and I are friends. I have a boyfriend."

The words put a smile on my face. Rusty knew how I felt about Sam, but he and Doug weren't out yet. Only a few people in town knew about their relationship. It meant a lot to me that he would tell Sam the truth to avoid hurting my chances.

Okay, Sam had two moms so he wasn't likely to freak out, but still. The gesture reminded me yet again how lucky I was to have Rusty as a friend.

Behind me, Sam exhaled slowly. When he spoke, he sounded calmer. "Thanks, Rusty. You didn't have to tell me that."

As I moved toward the store, Rusty's voice followed me. "Somehow, I think I did."

My steps lightened at the possible implications.

Downstairs, it only took a few minutes to get the store ready for the day. We were a few minutes past opening, but no customers waited outside. That was probably good, since anything unusual came across as big news in this town. After unlocking the doors, I stood by the register, staring at the rocking horse. It had been weird when I hadn't been able to get any reading off of it. But the fact that it shocked Olive? Something was wrong. Very wrong. Even though I'd only been psychic about a month, all six of my senses told me things didn't add up.

I couldn't leave the store, and I didn't know Mr. Patel's cell phone number to text, so I picked up the phone and called the magic shop.

A woman's voice answered on the second ring. "I've Put a Spell on You. This is Amira."

"Amira?" The excitement in my voice sprang forth. "I didn't know you were back in town! I'm so glad to hear your voice."

"Who is this?"

"Oh, sorry. Aly Reynolds. I moved next door to your parents a couple of weeks before you left, I think."

"Aly! How nice to hear from you. Yeah, after a year traveling around the world, I realized I couldn't outrun my broken heart. So I came back, more or less intact."

The magic shop's owner had taken a long sabbatical after a bad break-up. Since she left, her father had been running the store by appointment only, but he was the first to admit that he didn't have the same magical knowledge she did. He also owned a busy and popular restaurant in Willow Falls, so neither he nor his wife had the time to devote to keeping the store open full-time.

"Listen, I was going to get some advice from your dad, but honestly, you're a better person to ask." With a glance toward the back door, I lowered my voice in case Sam returned. "What could make an object shock someone?"

"I'm guessing you're not talking static electricity."

"You would be correct. Uh… a friend of mine was testing this particular object with her powers, and she fainted."

"Oh no! Is Olive okay?"

I tried not to laugh at her question. There really weren't

any secrets around here. "She's fine, I think. But I'd like to know what happened to her."

"It sounds like someone put a protective spell on whatever it is."

"Would a protective spell backfire like that?"

"Possibly," she said. "Depends on the parameters of the spell."

"Okay, but who would do that? And why?"

"Well, there are as many reasons to do a thing as there are people who might do it. To find the why, you need to find the witch."

Her words struck me like a bolt of lightning.

"A witch?"

"Well, yeah," she said. "It would have to be a witch. Where did you get this thing? That's your starting point."

My starting point. Mary. "Right. Of course. Thanks, Amira."

So Katrina's sister was a witch. Did she kill Katrina to keep her secret from coming out? Maybe the rocking horse contained multiple spells, a way of trying to figure out what we knew somehow. Or maybe she'd put listening spells on it to keep an eye on the family. Whatever it was, no way was this thing going into my house. Good thing I'd left it in my trunk overnight so Kevin wouldn't ask questions.

I hung up the phone in a daze. Instead of setting it down, I dialed Mary's number immediately. The call went straight to voice mail. I found myself wondering if she'd turned her phone off to avoid me. After hanging up, I sent a text thanking her again for the rocking horse and asking when I should return the pictures she'd loaned me. No reason to tip her off, but we definitely needed to chat. Then I dragged the rocking horse to the back room where Olive kept items not for sale and threw a sheet over it. Until I cleared things up, I didn't want that thing within a thousand feet of Kyle. I texted Olive to let her know, not expecting or getting a reply.

The rest of the morning dragged with the lack of customers and worrying about Olive. Sam didn't return to the shop, and I didn't think I should go up to the apartment to talk to Olive with him there. I did text Maria to make sure she knew what happened. She replied that she'd gone up through the back while I was on the phone. Sam was trying to insist on taking Olive to a doctor, so I left her alone.

Normally this empty store would be a great opportunity to work on homework, but when one of your professors gets murdered and your boss gets attacked helping you use your psychic powers to find a different killer, you don't super feel like thinking about physics or advanced biology.

To keep my mind occupied, I decided to see what I could find out about my suspects. Professor Zimm, according to Maloney College's website, had been working there for ten years. Professor Ng started eleven years ago, after spending five years at MIT. Yet Professor Zimm was the one offered tenure. How did Professor Ng feel about potentially losing out to someone younger and newer to teaching?

Some people posted every thought and reaction on social media for the world to see, but Professor Ng unfortunately wasn't one of them. From his pages, I gleaned that he enjoyed kayaking and gardening. Not a huge surprise that the botany professor liked to spend time outside.

According to an old article in the *Shady Grove Globe*, he'd been pressing the school for funds to build a greenhouse a few years ago after a wealthy town resident died and left a donation to the school. The article didn't give much detail, but a follow-up posted the next month showed that Dean Mendez spent the money on new equipment for the biology lab. Personally, I appreciated that, but suddenly I was seeing a lot of reasons Professor Ng might be happier with Professor Zimm out of the picture.

Since I was only twenty-one and never held a non-retail job, professional jealousy was beyond my sphere. Would getting overlooked for a grant make someone mad enough to kill? That was three years ago, before I even moved to town. But when you added tenure, suddenly it started to look a lot like I'd found a motive.

A motive and someone who would know that nature preserve inside and out.

CHAPTER SIXTEEN

TO MY SURPRISE, on Wednesday afternoon, Mr. Zimm called to ask if I was free to watch his kids after work. I hesitated. Yes, one hundred percent, I wanted to babysit if it meant going through their house and finding out who killed Professor Zimm. However, I also desperately wanted to rush home and practice scrying. This was the closest I'd ever been to finding Katrina's killer.

Eventually, I let Mr. Zimm know I'd be there. This could be my only chance to get into the Zimm house. If I said no, he might never ask again. Katrina had been dead for over a year. She wasn't going anywhere. Her story could wait. Finding Professor Zimm's killer couldn't. I didn't want to attend a school with a murderer running around—nor did I want my classmates in danger. Not even Tiffaneigh. Or probably not.

Also, I worked in an antique store. Sam was still upstairs with Olive, probably working there for the rest of the day. I didn't think he'd want to talk to me anytime soon. A sad thought, but yet another reminder that starting a relationship at the moment wasn't a great idea.

After a late morning rush of customers that lasted through the lunch hour, the store emptied out around two o'clock.

From experience, things usually didn't pick up until people finished work for the day and headed home. I could easily spend a couple of hours without many customers. Time to scry.

Missing Pieces sold dozens of mirrors, all sizes and shapes. A full-sized mirror by the dressing area appealed to me because it stood on large wooden feet, but it was too far from the front door. The bells over the door would jingle if anyone came in, but I might not hear, depending on my level of concentration. Ah, well. I didn't need that mirror.

Bigger wasn't necessarily better. We had a large selection of hanging wall mirrors, but most were too high up on the wall and/or too heavy for me to move on my own. Finally, I decided on a large silver hand mirror, a bit battered due to its age, but with a gorgeous ivy pattern etched on the back. The weight in my hand comforted me.

Scrying was a tricky business. My powers activated when I "used" an object that held imprints from a prior owner. Technically, scrying with a mirror meant using the mirror because I'd have to look into it. It would be tough to tell if I actually managed to get information from the scry, or if I was just having a regular vision. The difference being: with visions, thus far, the objects told me what they wanted me to know. I needed to scry the information *I* wanted.

If only Olive were around to talk me through it. But she needed to rest.

With a deep breath, I banished those thoughts. I could do this on my own, with a little help from my good friend Google. After about an hour skimming last night's search results a second time, I felt comfortable getting started.

First, tea. Not as part of the ritual, but to calm my nerves. Olive kept an electric kettle in the back room. The space was small, but it contained a counter with the essentials (i.e., a coffeemaker and phone charger).

After filling the kettle and flipping it on, I went back into the store and turned out the overhead lights. The store was naturally dim, due to the large bookcases and other items in front of the plate-glass windows blocking much of the sun from filtering in. Unfortunately, without lights I could barely see my hand in front of my face. After flipping them back on, I located a couple of old hurricane lamps and set them up on the floor near the front counter.

The lamps projected a nice circle of light without reflecting onto the surface of the mirror.

Perfect.

First, I settled onto the floor and crossed my legs. Closing my eyes, I counted to twenty and started reciting the elements of the periodic table to center myself.

The bells over the shop door rang. My eyes flew open. To my dismay, Thelma waltzed in.

"Why hello, dear! What are you doing? Holding a séance?" Her eyes darted around the room, missing nothing. "Are you talking to Professor Zimm? Tell Tammy I miss her!"

Mentally, I berated myself for not thinking to lock the door before getting started. Thinking quickly, I said, "No, um… Actually, Thelma, this is a little embarrassing. Can you keep a secret?"

Nope. Not even if her life depended on it.

"Of course, dear! Cross my heart."

"Well, it's just that, the guy who sold me this mirror said that if I looked into it in a dark room, I'd see the face of my true love." I bit my lip.

Her ears perked up at the potential to gain a bit of gossip. "I thought you were dating that boy at the coffee shop."

"No, we're just good friends. That's why I got this mirror. So far, though, I only see myself. Do you think I'm destined to be alone forever?"

Thelma rolled her eyes. "Oh, Aly. Don't tell me you got suckered by that mumbo jumbo! I expected better of you, dear girl."

I feigned embarrassment while thanking myself for having the foresight to turn the lights out. The harder it was to see my terrible acting job, the better.

"I know, I just…. Well, I've been lonely." I heaved a too-heavy sigh before pulling myself up and pasting on a bright smile. "Anyway, how can I help you, Thelma?"

"After seeing you at the funeral, I came in to see how you were doing." Translation: She wanted dirt.

"Thank you, but I'm fine. My heart goes out to Professor Zimm and her family." She waited expectantly, but I refused to give her anything resembling gossip. "Can I help you find something?"

When Thelma realized she wasn't going to get the dirt she sought, she vanished quicker than a stack of pancakes on Kyle's plate. Back to the mirror. At least the kettle boiled now. I'd almost forgotten about it.

Tea. Calming breaths. Incense. Low lights. Mirror. Remembering my lessons with Olive, I did some deep breathing to clear my mind, then gazed into the mirror, trying to let my eyes un-focus. To my surprise, something flickered across the surface.

This time, footsteps at the rear entrance drew me away from my task. Too late, I realized I didn't have any good excuse for what I was doing. "Aly? Why are all the lights out?"

Never did I think I'd be so disappointed to see Sam. Well, never before he walked in on me and Rusty and got upset. While part of my heart got excited at the notion that he did not like seeing me hug Rusty (and what that might mean), his words stung.

Too late, I realized that about fifteen seconds had passed since he asked the question. "Uh, the power blew?"

"That's weird. Everything is working upstairs. Did you check the fuse box?"

Immediately, I realized my mistake. Sam wasn't a random

customer or the town busybody. As the owners' son and the guy here to help, if we lost power, he'd take it upon himself to fix it. "Oh, sorry. No, it's fine. I was just testing something."

He tilted his head at me but didn't push. His decision to ignore the obvious lie only made me like him more.

"How's your mom?" I asked. "Did you need me to go get anything for her?"

"Mom insists she's doing fine. Won't tell me what happened, but I've learned not to push." To my surprise, he shuffled his feet and looked at the ground. "Look, Aly, I owe you an apology. When I saw Mom up there—it scared me."

"It scared me, too. That's why Rusty was comforting me. He's my best friend."

"I know," he said. "Well, I guess I know that now. Listen, it's none of my business who you date. After all, I live three hours away and you work for my mom..."

...and I adore you with every fiber of my being, I didn't say. I wanted to, but couldn't quite make the words come. Instead, I said, "Thanks. I know it looked bad."

"Let me make it up to you. We could get dinner tonight?"

Was that a hopeful note I heard in his voice? Nah, he was just probably one of those super nice people who couldn't stand knowing he'd hurt someone's feelings. But it wasn't like I'd turn him down just because it wasn't a date. The more time we spent together sans unconscious parent or murder accusations, the better.

"Yes!" The word ripped from my throat as if my heart spoke all by itself. I sighed when I remembered I wasn't available. "I mean, I'd love to, but I can't. I'm babysitting. Can I take a rain check?"

"Sure thing. Are you free tomorrow?"

For you? Yes., I didn't say. It wasn't a date. He said he wanted to talk about stuff. Probably store stuff. Or why his mom passed out in my arms. Not romantic stuff. Besides, he lived three hours away, as he pointed out. Dating with my powers could be weird. Even though I hadn't been on a date in over a year (and that barely counted, since it was Rusty just figuring out he wasn't attracted to women), I couldn't rush this.

I made a big show of checking the calendar on my phone so he wouldn't realize how uncool I was. "I've got class until four, but I'm free after that."

"Great. I'll pick you up at five-thirty. Text me your address?"

"Sounds good." I smiled brightly, hoping I looked casual. "It'll be fun."

"Then I guess it's a date." He grinned broadly at me, making my heart flip-flip before turning and heading back up to the family apartment.

As soon as the door shut behind him, I let out a squeal of joy. Finally!

CHAPTER SEVENTEEN

THE REST of the day was far less exciting. By the time Sam took over the store at five o'clock, my head ached from staring into a mirror in a dark room all afternoon. I'd gotten a few glimpses that told me not much, and I'd been interrupted roughly seven hundred times. The primary thing I learned was that teaching myself to scry in a public place was dumb.

After grabbing a sandwich from On What Grounds?, I drove straight to Professor Zimm's house. Even after a long day, I was energized by the thought of finding some clue as to what happened. According to the newspaper, she'd been shot, but I still had a million questions. Was she shot in her office or outside? Did she enter the nature preserve of her own initiative? If so, why? Were their tire tracks nearby?

Even if Mr. Zimm was the murderer, he probably knew enough not to keep the gun in their house after the fact. I didn't expect to find the murder weapon while watching the kids. But hopefully something would lead me to answers.

The Zimm home sat just over the border between Shady Grove and Willow Falls, probably about half an hour from the college. They lived in a quiet neighborhood, with trees lining the streets and houses set so far back from the road, I pitied the person who had to shovel those driveways. Then again, in a neighborhood like this, everyone either owned a snow blower or paid someone else.

In response to my knock, a boy who looked about eight appeared in the window beside the door. A moment later, a little girl stuck her nose to the glass several inches below them. The boy eyed me suspiciously.

"Who are you?" he demanded without opening the door.

I put on my friendliest smile. "My name is Aly, and I'm here to hang out with you for a bit. Is your dad around?"

In response, the girl shrieked. A shrill, piercing sound that made me want to put my hands over my ears. Good thing Kyle wasn't around. I never wanted him to hear that noise. Of course, if their dad was a murderer, better to reduce the number of children around him.

"We're not allowed to talk to strangers," the boy informed me solemnly.

Smart kid.

"Good thinking," I said. "Could you get your dad for me? Once he introduces us, we won't be strangers."

A steely glare was my only answer. As I looked at him, the resemblance to his mother made me sad. Same big brown eyes, same long nose, and rounded chin. Only the shape of his mouth reminded me of his father.

Small, shrill barks drew my attention to the bottom of the window. A tiny white puffball popped in and out of view, just barely.

"Killer, shh!" the boy said.

"Killer?" I asked. What was this place?

"Our dog," the girl informed me. "She's a Bichon Frisé."

I smiled at them. The dog's head still hadn't cleared the bottom of the windowsill. "Thanks for the warning."

Finally, as if I'd passed some test, the boy nodded. He turned and walked away. A few minutes later, Mr. Zimm rounded the corner and hurried to the door. Leaning down, he scooped up this tiny, squirming bundle of adorableness that must be Killer. She wore a giant pink polka dot bow on her collar, perhaps the only thing in the world that could make her look less vicious.

"I'm so sorry. I didn't hear you knock," he said. "Have you been here long?"

"Only a few minutes. Your kids kept me company. To be honest, I'm impressed they knew not to open the door."

"It took years of threats and child locks," he said with a wry smile. "Anyway, Aly, I'd like to introduce you to Davey and Martha. Oh, and Killer, of course."

"Davey, Martha, and I met on the porch," I said. "Hello, Killer. That's a big name for such a little dog."

"She has self-esteem issues," Mr. Zimm said. "Tabby thought a big name would make her feel better about herself."

That was so sweet, it made my heart ache. Even though I barely knew Professor Zimm, suddenly I missed her fiercely.

"I'm seven," Davey informed me, breaking the silence. "Martha is four. How old are you?"

"Twenty-one."

"That's old enough to vote!"

"Yes. Yes, it is."

"Do you vote?"

Before I could answer, Martha stepped forward, holding up a plastic baby with features so faded, it had to be an antique. "This is Dolly."

Leaning closer, I addressed the toy directly. "It's nice to meet you, Dolly."

The kids trailed behind while Mr. Zimm led me through the house, showing me the kitchen, the bathroom, the kids' bedrooms. He paused at a closed door and cleared his throat. "You, uh, shouldn't have a reason to go in there."

"That's Mommy's office," Davey informed me. "She died."

My heart broke for him all over again. Not only was he going to have to finish growing up without a mother, but he'd remember the pain of losing her. "I'm sorry, honey. Your mom was my teacher. She was a nice lady."

"Mama is in heaven!" Martha informed me. "With Grandpa."

Mr. Zimm shifted, clearly uncomfortable with the direction this conversation was going. Although he was one hundred percent wrong that I wouldn't have a reason to be going into his wife's office, I didn't want to seem too interested. Instead, I crouched down to address the little girl face-to-face.

"I hear heaven's a nice place," I said. "Have you had dinner yet?"

"I was just finishing up when you arrived," Mr. Zimm said. "Macaroni and cheese on the stove cooling, hot dogs are in the microwave. It beeped right after you rang the bell. I don't know if you've had anything but please, help yourself to whatever you like. I've got about forty frozen casseroles, and the kids won't eat anything with actual nutritional value."

I smiled at him. "I appreciate it, but I picked something up on the way. What about Killer? Has she eaten?"

"Killer eats raw," Mr. Zimm explained. "You don't need to worry about it."

"Raw? You mean raw meat? Like…chicken wings?" I didn't say it, but if they had a chest full of frozen meat at their disposal, that could explain the bones strewn around Professor Zimm's body.

Mr. Zimm misinterpreted my concerned look. "Yeah, but again, I fed her. And we don't give her live chickens or anything. Frozen food from the butcher. It's perfectly humane."

Right. I nodded, forcing myself to swallow my concerns. If

he was the killer, he couldn't know I was on to him. "Thanks. What time is bedtime?"

Ten minutes later, he was on his way with a backward glance over his shoulder that made me realize how much he hated leaving the kids. It surprised me how badly I didn't want Professor Zimm's husband to be the one who killed her.

As the kids were finishing dinner, my phone beeped with a text. My heart skipped a beat. Was it Sam, solidifying plans for our date? Just taking a moment to let me know he couldn't stop thinking about me?

But no, it was his mother.

Olive: *Look at you. You've got me texting.*

Me: *Does that mean You've been kidnapped?*

Olive: *Haha.*

Me: *Seriously, are you okay?*

Three dots indicating that she was composing an answer, then vanished, then returned. That made me more nervous.

My boss didn't text, she called, for the most part. It was annoying. The fact that she'd texted me for the first time on the day she got knocked out by a magical spell made me worry. At a minimum, she had something to say that couldn't wait until tomorrow, and she didn't want Sam to overhear.

I glanced at Davey, where he was now loading the plate he'd used into the bottom of the dishwasher. Martha still sat in her chair, feeding a hot dog to Dolly. Killer waited patiently on the floor, eyes glued to the girl's hand.

Finally, my phone buzzed.

Olive: *Maybe it's nothing, but ever since I woke up, I haven't felt like myself. I went downstairs and picked up the quill. It didn't tell me anything.*

I blinked at my screen several times. *Nothing?*

Olive: *Not even an inkling. So I walked around the shop, touching multiple items. Nothing. My gift is gone.*

Her words elicited a gasp out of me, so strong, both kids stopped what they were doing.

"I'm okay," I said. "Um…the dog startled me."

"Killer wouldn't hurt a fly," Martha said. "He only likes dead meat."

Yes, dead meat of the sort found strewn all around their mother's body. Was it a coincidence that the Zimm family and the murderer both had easy access to raw meat? Olive's problem called, but I wondered if the kids could tell me anything useful.

"Yeah, your dad mentioned that. He said you didn't feed her, but I bet you help him sometimes, right?"

"No. Only Daddy has a key to the freezer."

Interesting. Why lock the freezer? What else was in there?

Regretfully, I texted Olive that I would call her on the way home and put my phone away. At the moment, Professor Zimm needed me more.

The remainder of the evening was not nearly as eventful. Probably a mixed blessing when hanging out with children. Davey showed me a card game he played with his dad while Martha colored beside us. We tried to interest her in the game, but she preferred to draw.

When the time came, they went to bed so seamlessly, I wondered if Mr. Zimm had magic, too. After all, Kyle was pretty great, but we rarely got through bedtime without him asking for seven glasses of water and fifteen hugs first (then four trips to the potty).

I breathed a sigh of relief once Davey's bedroom door shut behind me. Martha was already in bed. Their father wasn't due back for at least an hour. Plenty of time to look through Professor Zimm's office for clues.

For ten minutes, I waited, needing to be one hundred percent sure the kids were asleep before making my move. The last thing I wanted was for one of them to catch me going through their mom's stuff. Finally, when the soft sounds of slow breathing filtered through both doors, I tiptoed down the hall, saying a silent prayer that the office wouldn't be locked.

It wasn't. The handle turned silently, and the door swung open. I didn't feel a switch beside the door, but light from the street filtered in through the open window. Not much, but enough to navigate around the furniture.

In stark contrast to her office at the university, chaos reigned inside this room. Papers, post-it notes, pens, and other stuff covered every square inch of the desk. Overflowing bookcases lined one wall, with some books haphazardly pulled out and left open. Every drawer in the desk had been pulled open.

What the heck was going on?

I stood in the center of the room, turning slowly for a long time before it hit me. Of course. Evidence. Police would have taken Professor Zimm's computer for evidence, along with any papers or anything else that might give some clue who had killed her. I should've known. Even though she (probably) didn't die here, police would have wanted to investigate the home. They must have created this mess when they searched, and Mr. Zimm hadn't cleaned up yet. Maybe the officers hadn't gotten a chance to go through her on-campus office when I broke in. That would explain the difference.

Not quite willing to give up, I wheeled the desk chair back to its usual spot, taking careful note of exactly how I'd found it. Then I sat, facing the desk, pretending to be sifting through a pile of papers.

Nothing happened.

My gifts weren't well-defined, and I still only had a very basic handle on how to get them working. The good news was, from this vantage point, I spotted a bookcase behind the door that I hadn't seen in the low light. Police apparently hadn't been interested in biology, because the shelf overflowed with old textbooks, on topics ranging from Genetics to Cell Adhesion and more.

Also one on…rebuilding a 1957 Chevrolet? That wasn't science-y at all. Not that a woman couldn't have varied interests, but it seemed out of place on the second shelf, stuck at the end of a row of books authored by Professor Zimm herself. Curious, I pulled it out with one finger, noting that the book seemed oddly light for something with a three-inch spine.

Once, a used book sent me a vision of the prior owner. What were the odds of lightning striking twice?

The front cover fell open, revealing that the book was hollow. Someone had glued the pages together, then carefully cut a hole in the middle. A gun-shaped hole, currently empty.

Professor Zimm owned a gun. For some reason, that possibility never occurred to me. Was she afraid of someone? Did she have a permit? Why wasn't it here? The article I'd read in the *Shady Grove Globe* didn't mention a gun at the scene, but police possibly wouldn't want that detail published. I didn't even know if her purse had been found with her.

Had it been Professor Zimm's own gun that killed her?

If Professor Zimm had been afraid of someone, maybe she'd taken the gun out of its hidey hole and started to carry it around with her. Since she had two little kids, she also could have done that six years ago and bought a safe or taken the gun to work or even gotten a carry permit. Since the book wasn't talking, there was no way to know without asking Mr. Zimm. I didn't want to do that until I was certain he wasn't the one who killed her.

I wondered how to work that into a conversation. *Hey, Aly, how were the kids?*

Great! Did you by any chance murder your wife? Also, do you know where her missing gun is?

Could the gun be in the freezer?

It took me about three seconds of staring at an array of fish sticks, chicken nuggets, and popsicles to realize that the locked freezer mentioned by the kids wasn't the one standing in the kitchen. They must have a spare somewhere. I guessed the garage because that's where people in California kept spare freezers.

I guessed wrong.

Professor Zimm's car was there, though, or a car I assumed to be hers. A black Honda Pilot with tinted windows. Enough dirt to make me wonder if she went four-wheeling. Doors locked. I made a mental note to look for the keys after I found the freezer. Then I remembered that this was the East Coast, not California, and people here had basements for things like storing their extra food.

Five minutes later, I found my way to the bottom of the basement stairs and flipped on the lights. Bingo! The freezer sat in the corner. With a nervous glance at the ceiling, I moved toward it. Hopefully the garage door would open loudly when Mr. Zimm got home, because I couldn't think of any explanation for being here if he caught me snooping.

The key to the freezer hung on a hook beside it. Martha must not realize that the only people her dad wanted to keep out of it were under five feet tall.

Any hopes of finding something of interest inside dwindled when I realized that if Mr. Zimm was hiding evidence of a murder, he probably would have moved the key. Still, I twisted the key in the lock and lifted the lid.

As expected, rows of frozen meat lay inside. Whole chickens, whole turkeys, and lots of stuff I couldn't identify. It didn't matter. I shifted some of the packages aside, but the only thing of interest was the three containers of triple brownie fudge ice cream hidden at the bottom. My stomach suggested I "search" them for clues, but I didn't want to advertise my presence. After locking the freezer, I replaced the key exactly where I'd found it and pondered my next step.

A lot of people who kept a gun in the home for protection

put it in a nightstand. Or so I'd read in books. Off the top of my head, I couldn't think of anywhere else the gun might be unless Professor Zimm had it with her when she died. Unfortunately, there was no way around the fact that I was going to have to invade the Zimms' privacy a little bit more. Time to search the primary bedroom.

Back on the top floor, I found the room easily. There were only four doors, and I'd already been in both kids' bedrooms and the bathroom. A massive four-poster bed sat in the middle of the room, probably king-sized. On the right side, the blue-patterned comforter lay pristine, as if no one had ever slept on it. The right-hand nightstand top was mostly clear, with only a small lamp and a glasses case on the surface. Since both Professor Zimm and her husband wore glasses, I couldn't be sure who slept on that side.

The other side presented a series of opposites: comforter flung back haphazardly, pillows crisscrossed like the occupant had trouble sleeping. The adjacent table groaned under the weight of a massive stack of books. A tissue box, over-the-counter medications, pens, and other random stuff covered the rest of the surface. Moving closer, I peered at the books: a mix of fiction and non-fiction. Memoirs from a Hollywood actor and a Supreme Court Justice. Murder mysteries and Regency romance. Bookmarks stuck out from about four of them.

Books that, if I guessed correctly, no one would ever finish reading.

My gut told me that this side belonged to my professor, that her husband hadn't even been able to make her side of the bed after she died. My heart broke at the realization that he'd preserved the room exactly the way she left it. Score one point for "not a murderer."

I couldn't bring myself to lie on the bed to induce a vision. Casually, I picked up one of her books and flipped through it, but nothing happened. Grabbing a tissue, I wiped my nose, not expecting it to tell me anything. It didn't. Next, I picked up a pen and pretended to scribble a note on the tissue. It ripped, and the pen told me nothing.

There had to be something around here to tell me what I wanted to know. I didn't particularly want to put Professor Zimm's clothes on, but it beat crawling beneath the sheets. Before crossing that line, I headed for the attached bathroom.

Oh, man. My jaw dropped at the site of the massive tub filling the room. It looked glorious. A person could swim laps in that thing. You needed to *climb and descend stairs* to get into it. For a heartbeat, I hoped Professor Zimm once had a major moment occur in her bathtub and that I could relive it by climbing on in.

A heavy sigh escaped me. That was a terrible idea for many reasons, but even if it weren't, the bathtub shared a wall with Davey's room. I couldn't risk the running water waking him up. With one last look of longing, I headed for the closet.

The Zimms had a fairly standard walk-in, with a neat, orderly row of suits and button-up shirts organized by color on one-side and random clothes stuffed onto hangers on the other. Across the back wall, a row of costumes drew me in. Thor. Black Widow. Wonder Woman. She-Ra. Apparently the Zimms liked to cos-play.

Time to go. This wasn't telling me anything, and I felt gross digging through their stuff. All I wanted to do was go home, take a shower, and curl up on the couch with a good book. There was zero chance I was going to put on anything Professor Zimm owned and trigger a vision. I'd find another way.

A cough from the front of the closet made me jump a mile. I spun around, praying it would be Martha or Davey. No such luck. A squeak escaped me.

Mr. Zimm stood in the doorway.

CHAPTER EIGHTEEN

THE BLOOD DRAINED OUT of my face, leaving me light-headed. We stared at each other. I'd been caught red-handed, and we both knew it. My initial instinct was to run. Flee down the stairs and out of the house. He probably wouldn't leave the kids alone to follow and kill me.

Unfortunately, Mr. Zimm stood between me and the door. The only option was to bluff my way out of this. "You're home early! Did you have a nice evening?"

"Yeah, it was great. Nothing beats being the guy whose wife just got murdered at a work event."

Touché. I didn't know what to say to that. A nervous laugh escaped me. "You're probably wondering—"

"Cut the crap, Aly, we both know what you're doing."

We did? Great, he was going to call the cops on me. He probably thought I was trying to steal something. Or he realized I was onto him, and he was going to kill me and feed me to the coyotes, covered in Killer's raw chicken parts.

Why, oh why, did I come here alone?

"I swear, it's not what it looks like." I began, trying to figure out how to inch toward the door without getting any closer to Mr. Zimm. Maybe I could lock myself in the bath-room and call 911?

"Oh, I think it is." He took three long steps forward, grip-ping me by the forearms. His eyes were wild.

I flinched and tried to jerk away, but he held fast. "Please. You don't have to do this."

When he spoke, desperation filled his voice. "Did you have a vision? Do you know who killed my Tabby?"

At Mr. Zimm's words, I choked. "You know what I can do?"

"Tabby figured it out," he said. "She was very intuitive."

"I don't understand," I said. "How?"

"Come on. Let's get out of my bedroom closet. I'll make some coffee, and we can chat."

Until he mentioned that, I had almost forgotten that we stood about fifteen feet from the bed he'd once shared with my now dead-professor. Awkward city, especially if one of the kids woke up and found us in here. Not to mention that Mr. Zimm still topped my suspect list. The fact that he somehow learned about my powers didn't exonerate him. He could just be trying to find out what I knew before he decided whether to kill me, too.

This had been a terrible idea. I shifted from one foot to the next, wondering about my chances of getting out the front door before he attacked me.

"Look, I know what you're thinking," he said. "If I can prove I didn't kill my wife, will you calm down?"

"Yes? I mean, yes, definitely, that would make me feel better. But how?"

"Easy," he said. "I'm going to give you a vision."

My mouth dropped open. I didn't quite believe what I was hearing. This could be astonishingly good luck—or a painful misunderstanding. "You're going to show me your wife's death?"

He sighed heavily. "I wish. No, but I can show you it wasn't me." He unlocked his phone and handed it to me.

Without a moment's hesitation, I took the device. The home screen showed over four hundred unread texts and more than a thousand unread emails, which made me twitch. Those big red numbers made me more uncomfortable than getting caught digging through his stuff. I landed firmly on Team Zero Inbox. Of course, I'd never lost a spouse.

Opening a new text message, I typed in my number. Then I nearly dropped the phone as the world twisted under me.

A voice in my ear droned on. I hadn't heard a word the man said after, "We have reason to believe your wife has been killed."

I sank into the desk chair, a short-backed, orange-brown seat with two arms and wheels. The spindly desk wasn't made for the pile of books and binders stacked on it for this conference. It didn't matter. Nothing mattered.

My eyes landed on the binder leaning against the wall. "Welcome to the Indianapolis Garden Heights Business Center." A hotel in Indiana. Nowhere near Shady Grove.

My voice shook when I spoke. Deeper than usual, not me. "Are you sure it's my Tabby?"

In my ear, someone said, "I think so. We got the preliminary ID from the girl who found her. But it would help if we could get something with your wife's fingerprints on it to confirm. When was the last time you spoke with Tabitha?"

"Yesterday evening. She was planning to spend about an hour researching before a late appointment."

"Do you know who she was seeing?"

"Nah. She said she had some flim-flam meeting."

"Excuse me?"

"A fancy word for bull. We don't like to cuss in front of the children. I'm afraid it's caught on."

"Oh, I see." The voice was so full of compassion, it took me a minute to recognize it as belonging to Tim Matthews. "How did she seem?"

"Normal. Office hours can be the worst part of the job. So many unreasonable requests. She rarely complained, though." Panic filled my chest. "The kids. Where are Davey and Martha?"

"They're fine, sir. Spent last night at a sleepover."

A flood of relief made my body sink back into the chair. "Thank goodness. I forgot."

"Understandable, under the circumstances. If you speak to your wife, please let us know as soon as possible. Maybe it's not her."

The despair filling me said it was. This was the first morning since we got married that Tabby didn't text hello during my travels. "Thank you, Sheriff Matthews. I'll be on the next flight back to Shady Grove."

The phone call ended, and the phone dropped onto the desk. The room blurred as I dissolved into sobs.

When I came back to myself, Mr. Zimm watched me, a host of emotions playing across his face. This was the first time I'd intentionally induced a vision in front of the person I wanted to read, and I felt a weird connection with him. "I'm so sorry, Mr. Zimm."

His lips curved upwards in a sardonic half-smile. "Please. After that, I think you can call me Ethan."

"Ethan. Let's chat." He still hadn't mentioned how he knew about my abilities. I made the universal "after you" motion and followed him down the stairs to the kitchen.

"You seem awfully relaxed," he commented as he gestured for me to sit on a stool at the island. Killer sniffed my feet as if to reprimand me for being where I shouldn't have gone. "I guess you believe me now?"

"This feels like a test," I said, leaning down to pat the dog's head. "I know you didn't do it because when you handed me your phone, I had a vision of Sheriff Matthews calling you with the news."

"Smart. You passed." His smile faded. "Sorry to have you live through such a painful moment."

"It's okay," I said. "I suppose you could've hired someone

to kill her while you were out of town, but your shock and pain felt genuine. Again, I'm so sorry for your loss. I liked your wife."

"Thank you." With a tight smile, he turned his attention to the cupboards. "You can probably call her Tabitha, too."

I wouldn't, but I appreciated the gesture. While Ethan made coffee and offered me an enormous slice of chocolate cake—which I happily accepted, of course—I explained everything that happened so far. When I got to the part about Professor Ng getting tenure, he almost dropped his plate.

"Gary? You think Gary killed Tabby? No way."

"You know him?"

"Of course I do," he said. "Maloney College isn't that big. Tabby graduated from here, you know. Years ago. They both did. They even dated briefly when he was in grad school, before he went off to MIT. He's been a friend for decades."

"But he had motive and opportunity. He's teaching all of her classes, which has to come with more pay. Plus, she was going to beat him for tenure *and* got the funding he wanted a couple of years ago. He knows the nature preserve inside and out. Everything adds up."

"Professor Ng's specialty is botany. He hates cellular biology and chemistry. He would be perfectly happy to never teach either," Ethan insisted. "Gary just wants to dig in the dirt. Also, more work at a small college doesn't necessarily translate to more pay."

I sighed. "Well, he was my best suspect."

"I'm not going to tell you to stop looking into what happened. I need to know, and police still haven't found the gun. But Gary's a pacifist. Ran for State Assembly a few years back. His entire platform revolved around abolishing the Second Amendment."

"Really?"

"Really. Sorry to break it to you, Aly, but Gary's not our guy."

Instead of answering, I took another bite of cake. Being anti-gun did not mean a person was incapable of murder under the right circumstances. Also, people change. But I could see trying to convince Ethan would be a waste of time —especially when I didn't have any real evidence. Professor Ng may have a motive, and the fact that he worked with Professor Zimm probably gave him opportunity, but those two things didn't necessarily make someone a killer.

That reminded me, though. "Speaking of guns—did Professor Zimm carry one? I found that empty book in your office."

He smiled. "No. She inherited that book from her dad. Kept it as a reminder, but we didn't take the gun itself. Never wanted the thing in the house with the kids, you know."

I understood, but now I was down two suspects (if Ethan was right about Professor Ng) and a murder weapon. Since Brad and Tiffaneigh were together, either they'd teamed up to kill Professor Zimm, or I was back at square one. This evening wasn't turning out to be as fruitful as I'd hoped. So far, the only thing I'd learned was that Ethan knew about my abilities.

"How did you find out about me?" I asked. "You said your wife mentioned it, but I never told her. To be honest, I'm surprised a science professor would believe in mystical powers."

"As unusual as a biology major who has visions?" My lips twitched in response, but I let him continue without interrupting. "I was as surprised as you, the first time she told me. The entire subject fascinated her, though. Tabby had been doing a lot of research, long before we met. Tracking, looking at genomes. She suspected supernatural abilities are found in a recessive gene mutation."

Huh. When I'd first had a vision, I'd been completely freaked out at the thought that everything I knew about science was wrong, that mysticism might be every bit as real.

I wished I could've gotten a chance to talk to another scientist who believed. "That's fascinating. I'd love to see her research. I mean, if you'd be comfortable showing it to me."

"She'd like that," he said wistfully, taking a long swallow of coffee while staring absently away from me. "Maybe you'll use it once you get your degree."

Or in my master's thesis, when the time came. There was a fascinating concept. The possibilities thrilled me. "What got her interested in supernatural abilities? It's kind of an out-there subject."

"Not for her. Tabby was a reader," he said.

"She liked books about psychics?" Obviously. Who didn't?

"Ha. No. Well, I mean, yes, but that's not what I meant. She read people's auras. Not like what you'd see in the movies, but she sensed a few things. For one, she knew when someone was Gifted. She spotted it the second she met you and your nephew at the bookstore. I remember when she came home that night, she told me she'd never met someone so young with such a strong aura."

The words made me feel oddly proud, as if I had anything to do with the strength of my aura. "I'm surprised you remembered."

"Well, you don't exactly have a common name." I cringed, and he continued, "I was glad you approached me at the funeral because I didn't need to come up with some pretext for inviting you over. Imagine if I'd called you out of the blue, a total stranger, and invited you to come poke around my house."

"I'd have been ecstatic," I said truthfully. "Okay, well, maybe ecstatic and weirded out."

He laughed. "Did you find anything? Any clues?"

"Sorry, no." I gestured toward the office. "It probably would've helped if I could've gotten here before the police did. They made such a mess, it would take me hours to find anything useful. Assuming they didn't take it."

He set his coffee cup down on the counter and tilted his head at me. "What are you talking about?"

"The desk. Papers everywhere. Total chaos."

Mr. Zimm laughed. "That's just Tabby. Police didn't search our house because there's no evidence this is where she was killed, and I was out of town when it happened. I'm afraid the office always looks like that. Drove me crazy, but what are you going to do?"

"Why would she keep her home office such a disaster and her office at school so neat?"

"She wouldn't. Her place on campus was just as bad," he said. "She swore she knew where everything went, but it always looked like a hurricane hit it to me."

"No, it didn't. I was there last week, and it was spotless." Realization slowly dawned. Someone had cleaned up Professor Zimm's office, but it wasn't her.

CHAPTER NINETEEN

BY THE TIME I got home that night, I was exhausted, but I had one more thing to do before collapsing into bed. My brother sat on the living room couch, watching television. Perfect. After a long week of drafting legal documents and offering pro bono advice to people charged with violent crimes throughout the greater Capital Region, my brother liked to chill on the couch with the TV and some paperwork. As expected, his laptop sat open on the cushion beside him, and papers spread along the surface.

He sat up when I entered. "Do you want to sit down? I can clean up a bit."

I pretended to consider his offer. "What are you watching?"

"Mets vs. Red Sox, 1986."

"How many times have you watched that game? It was before I was born."

"Look, there aren't that many Mets World Series games to choose from. How many times have you watched that movie about the kissing booth?"

A lot. It wasn't worth arguing, because I needed my brother to stay distracted. I'd arrived home shortly after nine-thirty, and the game on the TV was entering the third inning. Meaning there should be plenty of time for him to fall asleep and for me to implement my plan before he woke up and moved into his room.

"Touché. Anyway, thanks for the offer, but I'm beat. I'm going to do some homework and then crash."

"Night, Aly."

"Night, Kev."

Once upstairs, I changed into my jammies, then went into the bathroom to brush my teeth and wash my face as usual. Although Kevin probably wasn't paying any attention to me from his spot on the couch, I didn't want him to notice anything remotely out of the ordinary.

It was time to finish this, once and for all. That mirror was going to tell me what happened to Katrina. I would make it tell me.

Ten minutes later, candles sat strategically placed around the room. Once I got the mirror set up, I'd light them. A stick of incense burning on the window sill relaxed me somewhat. A cracked window would let out any smoke without setting off the fire alarm, hopefully also without making me freeze to death. My tablet stood between two candles, displaying an old picture from Kevin and Katrina's wedding that I'd pulled off Facebook.

Only one thing left to do: get the mirror from underneath Kevin's bed, smuggle it into my room, and remove the wrapping without him hearing me. No problem.

Wiping my sweaty palms on my pants, I tiptoed to the top of the stairs. The sportscaster's banter filled the silence, but underneath I heard another, more welcome sound: the soft, rhythmic breathing of a person who had fallen asleep watching television.

Here goes nothing.

With one last look toward the couch, I moved toward Kevin's room and opened the door silently on the hinges.

Hardly daring to breathe, I crossed over to the bed, lowered myself to one knee, and reached for the brown paper.

When my fingers closed around the mirror's frame, I almost cheered. Some small part of my mind worried Kevin would have figured out my plan and moved the mirror before I got a chance. (Impossible unless he also had powers, but you never knew.) An inch at a time, I slid it toward me, creeping backward along the floor as I went.

The mirror was a bit bulky, but not heavy. Once the far edge cleared the underside of the bed, I hefted it up and returned to the door. If I ran into Kevin now, there was no possible way to explain my situation. You don't graduate Columbia Law School and get a big-firm New York City job making about a jillion dollars a year without being able to draw obvious conclusions.

Luckily, the sound of Kevin's slow breathing followed me back to my room. As soon as the door clicked into place behind me, I sagged with relief. Once I flipped the lock, nothing could stop me.

I was going to get the truth.

First, I unwrapped the mirror and put it on the floor in the middle of the room. The candles had been strategically placed to provide illumination, but not to flicker on the surface. Moving around the room, I lit each one before snapping my lights off and settling cross-legged onto the floor.

Staring at Katrina's picture, I took multiple deep breaths. I cleared my mind, focusing on nothing but being calm and open. My nose itched.

No. I banished the thought and started over.

In, out.

In, out.

When I felt calm, I closed my eyes and quietly repeated a chant I'd found on the internet and tailored to meet my needs. Three times, breathing slowly and steadily. Then, picturing Katrina firmly in my mind, I opened my eyes and gazed into the mirror.

At first, nothing happened. My eyes were too focused. After a moment, my vision softened, and the mirror's surface started to waver.

"Show me," I whispered. "Show me Katrina. How did she die? Who killed her?"

The mirror grew murky. Bracing myself, I leaned forward. To my surprise, an image appeared on the surface.

Katrina exited a room at the top of the stairs, closing the door behind her. "Have a good nap, baby."

The sight of her short honey-colored hair, lululemon leggings, and kind face made my heart ache. She stopped short at the top of the stairs, her mouth opened into an "O" shape. "What do you want?"

"You know what I want." The voice was pitched low, raspy. It almost sounded like it was full of static. No way I'd recognize the voice if I heard it again. "I need you."

"I'm not going with you. No way." She moved silently down the stairs, keeping her voice low, as if she were afraid to wake Kyle. While I appreciated the concept of never waking a sleeping child, I needed the other person in the room to speak up. They must be standing in front of the door, but from the vantage point of the mirror, I couldn't see anything but a black-clad elbow and the curve of a hip. It could have been almost anyone. "You need help."

"I need you to stop concealing who you are. If we combine powers—"

"Stop it! Stop that!" Katrina raised her hands, waving them in the air. "I don't have any powers. You need to go."

"You can deny it, but I've been getting a very strong reading from this house."

"Strong readings?"

"Psychic energy," the person said. "And I know it's not your husband, so don't lie to me."

Katrina swallowed. The blood drained from her face.

I gasped. She must've reached the same realization I did—that there was someone in the house with powers, and it wasn't her or Kevin.

"Okay, you've got me. I'll go with you. Let me just leave a note for my husband. Please."

"So you can tell him about me? Don't be daft."

"I won't, I promise. He just needs to know not to try to find me. If we do this, I can't come back."

In the corner of the mirror, I saw the person wave a hand dismissively. "Do whatever you need to do."

Katrina strode directly toward the mirror, her blue eyes meeting mine in a way that almost jolted me out of the image. But it was an illusion. She couldn't see me. "There's a pen and paper right here."

She stopped and opened the drawer in the table. Then, she stepped back and yanked. In one fluid motion, she spun and threw the drawer at the person in the doorway. They grunted, and something clattered to the floor. Probably the drawer. At the same moment, Katrina grabbed a large vase from the table and turned. She swung wildly, sending water and flowers scattering.

The person stepped into view, a blur of black hoodie and sunglasses. Pale skin, maybe? I gritted my teeth in frustration. In the mirror, the figure reached up, effortless taking the vase from Katrina's hands. They wore gloves, which wasn't helpful, but appeared to be shorter than Katrina. Lean.

Hold on. Something peeked out between the glove and the cuff of the hoodie. A tattoo? I moved closer, desperate for any clue.

The vase shattered to the ground, and my concentration wavered. The vision flickered, and I struggled to focus.

"Signs of a struggle," the police report had said. Now I understood.

The person wrapped their arms around Katrina. I needed to see who it was! The sleeve of the hoodie shifted, revealing a wavy line. Definitely a tattoo. It was dark green, not the right color for a scar. The bits I saw curved around the skin. A vine? As they struggled, the patch of skin moved out of my sight.

Katrina whispered, "Please."

The mirror clouded over.

Squeezing my eyes shut, I shook my head to get the image out of my mind. I couldn't breathe. Couldn't think. All I saw was Katrina, murdered to stop someone from finding out the truth about Kyle. I still didn't have any idea who that person was.

Desperate to clear my head, I blew out all the candles and threw the window open. A blast of cold wind rocketed around the room, but I welcomed the exterior chill. Anything beat the sudden coldness inside of me.

Not feeling confident that I'd manage to return the mirror to Kevin's room without dropping it, I shoved the blasted thing under my bed. Just in time, too, because a second later, someone knocked on my door.

"Is everything okay in there? I heard a scream."

Oops. Good thing I didn't wake Kyle.

Plastering a smile on my face, I opened the door a few inches. "Sorry. Just watching an old season of *Scream Queens*. I love this show."

He gave an exaggerated shudder. "I don't see the appeal. Turn it down, would you?"

"Yeah, sorry. I thought my earbuds were in."

It was a true mark of how exhausted Kevin must be that he didn't point out what a stupid thing that was to say. I sucked at lying under pressure. "No problem. I'll see you in the morning. Enjoy the blood and gore."

I closed the door quickly before turning and resting my head against the wood. There certainly had been a lot of blood and gore in my life lately. But I didn't enjoy any of it.

CHAPTER TWENTY

MOLECULAR BIOLOGY and chemistry had been canceled, but my other classes continued, so I still had to go to campus on Thursday morning. What I really wanted was to get back inside Professor Zimm's office for a second look. The administration building would be unlocked since it was open to students during the day, but it would also be busy enough that someone might see me going where I didn't belong.

Suddenly, I had an idea. I texted Ethan, and he replied immediately. Five minutes after my last seminar ended, Dean Mendez met me at the door of Professor Zimm's office holding a stack of empty cardboard boxes. "Aly! How lovely of you to volunteer to collect Tabby's belongings for her husband."

I nodded. "Mr. Zimm was so upset. I thought it might help him to have someone separate her personal effects from the research and stuff, so he doesn't have to do it."

She nodded. "One of your classmates offered to do it for extra credit, but that's not how we operate around here."

I stifled the urge to ask if it had been Tiffaneigh. That girl would do anything for an A. You almost had to respect her tenacity.

Inside the office, everything looked the same as the first time I'd been here. Not a slip of paper out of place: a stark contrast to Professor Zimm's home office, closet, and bedroom. Now that I knew how she normally kept things, it was clear someone else had been in here.

Turning to the door, I called Dean Mendez back. "Does the college have cleaning staff?"

"We do."

"Do they tidy up these offices? Put books away and stuff?" At her confused look, I said, "Um, the office is just surprisingly neat."

"Tidy? They do the floors and empty trash, but Tabitha would have strung up anyone who touched her papers. She had a 'system', you see." Dean Mendez stepped into the office, frowning. She looked around. "The office hasn't looked like this since the day she moved in."

"Do you think any of her TAs would have come in to clean after she died?"

"Maybe if they needed something to continue her research. But they should have called me first. This is very unsettling."

"How many assistants did she have?" Anyone who worked with Professor Zimm could have useful information for me.

"Only two. Isaac was in Rochester with the basketball team for the weekend, and he hasn't been back on campus that I know of. Very upset."

Hmmm. Another link to Brad. "Her TA played on the team?"

"No, he traveled with the team. School mascot." She thought for a minute. "Now that I think about it, Tabby's other assistant dropped out at the semester break. Sick family member or something. Excuse me, I need to make some calls."

As soon as Dean Mendez shut the door, I slid into the desk

chair and texted Ethan again for Professor Zimm's login information. Seconds later, the computer let me in, and I waited as her calendar filled the screen. Surely he wouldn't have sent that information if he were working with the killer.

The calendar itself held no surprises. Other than her regular classes and lab time, she'd noted a dentist appointment on Monday, check-ups for the kids Wednesday afternoon. Friday office hours, four to six pm, just like Ethan said. No student meetings on the schedule. Someone must have dropped in.

Shifting gears, I went over to her email. Unlike her husband, Professor Zimm had very few unread messages, and all of them came in since she'd died. Not surprisingly, there was no "Here's why I killed you!" message. I scrolled back through a couple of days, looking to see if she'd been arguing with anyone, but the inbox was sparse, especially compared to her husband's. Apparently, Professor Zimm didn't see the need to keep many old messages. Or whoever had cleaned up the office had also cleared out her inbox.

I was about to give up when a small number (1) drew my attention to the Drafts folder. Had Professor Zimm been writing an email before she died?

The message was short and unhelpful, written at nine-thirty in the morning. *Pray for me. I've got another BS meeting later.* Ah, yes. The "flim-flam" Ethan referred to. A word to add to my Kyle-safe vocabulary. From the tone, I guessed the email was going to either Ethan or another professor, but the message was unaddressed and never sent. Not helpful.

She couldn't have been more specific? "I have a meeting with Tiffaneigh, who is going to murder me if I don't give her an A."

Okay, I didn't think she did it, not after our talk in the coffee shop. But what kind of meeting constituted a "BS" meeting? Someone wanting to challenge the syllabus? Ask for an accommodation? Brad Stevens had been high on my list of suspects, but after my vision the other day, he couldn't have done it. The timing didn't match up. If he'd had a meeting with Professor Zimm, it must've been long before she died.

All those thoughts swirled around in my head as I logged out of the computer and finished searching the office. Nothing else of interest jumped out at me. If the killer had taken Professor Zimm from her office, they'd done a great job of cleaning up after themselves. At this rate, we'd never know who did it.

In case I ran into Dean Mendez on the way out, I quickly filled a box with stuff Ethan might want to have, plus some research that might be related to her paranormal studies. Then I headed for my car.

"Aly! Wait up!" At the sound of my name, I stopped and looked around.

Tiffaneigh caught up with me and tugged my hand, pulling me to one side of the path. "Come on."

"Where are we going?"

"Shh."

Not knowing what else to do, I followed her down the path from the science building, still carrying the awkward but not heavy box. We wound around campus. It wasn't for several minutes that I noticed the man moving briskly, several yards in front of us. I caught up to her and lowered my voice. "Are you following Professor Ng?"

"Not if you're so loud he catches us," she said pointedly. "Look, you're my cover. If he spots me alone, it's more suspicious than if we're out here together, gathering samples for our botany class."

"We don't have a botany class together."

"He doesn't know that."

As the botany professor, he might, but it wasn't worth arguing. Professor Ng remained my primary suspect, despite Ethan's refusal to consider him. If following him might help me find some actual evidence, I was one hundred percent in.

Tiffaneigh and I moved together, away from the center of campus, across the parking lot. Professor Ng went to the back of a Toyota RAV4 and opened the trunk. My arms were starting to ache.

"Are we supposed to get in a car and tail him wherever he might go?"

"If it comes to that."

"Your car's a bit flashy for tailing someone, don't you think?"

"Why do you think I grabbed you?" she asked reasonably. "But hold on."

Professor Ng removed his pristine khaki coat and laid it gently in the backseat of his car. Then he grabbed a black overcoat and pulled it on. An old-beat-up coat. Exactly the type that might be missing a button. Then he grabbed something out of the SUV and shut the back, once again on the move.

A shovel. Professor Ng kept a shovel in his car.

"Can I please put this box down?"

Tiffaneigh sighed and pulled out her key fob. "My trunk's right here. Hurry."

Although I was dying to examine the back of her car for clues, I didn't dare risk her wrath. The box went into the trunk, and I silently closed the lid. Thanks, Kevin, for drilling into me the need to be gentle with an expensive car.

Without another word, Tiffaneigh and I headed across the parking lot. Our pace remained steady. Professor Ng walked as if he'd followed this path dozens of times. It took me a minute to realize that we were approaching the Nature Preserve from a different direction than the one Kevin and I had taken the day we found Professor Zimm's body. Julie's words came back to me: several of the trails were wide enough for someone to drive a small SUV on them. A small SUV like the one Professor Ng drove.

A small gasp escaped me.

"Glad you finally caught up with me," Tiffaneigh said.

"Okay, but why are we following him? This is a public place. Maybe he walks the Nature Preserve every day. He is the botany professor, after all."

"Maybe so. That would help him know the best places to bury a body, wouldn't it?"

"To be fair, the spot he chose wasn't actually the best—" At her withering glare, I swallowed the rest of my sentence. "Good point."

Tiffaneigh studied the path, the trees, and the sky. After a couple of minutes, she finally said, "Is he heading for the spot where you found Professor Zimm?"

I considered her words for a moment before answering. "I'm not sure. This isn't where Kevin and I entered the preserve. We found her on an offshoot of the blue trail. But I know most of the trails cross at some point."

She pointed to an arrow on a nearby tree. "This is the red trail, which connects to the blue trail in about a quarter mile, I think."

Clearly, she knew the preserve much better than I did. Then again, I'd only been a student for two weeks and I'd spent half that time investigating a murder.

Sure enough, after a few more minutes, Professor Ng chose a fork in the trail that sent him following the blue arrows. Thankfully, he didn't turn to look over his shoulder at any point. But I still didn't have the slightest clue where we were relative to the scene of the crime.

The trees were thick here, making it difficult to see anyone ahead. A dark-haired man didn't exactly stand out in the shadows. The beat-up black coat didn't help. But the question remained: was it missing a button?

After another ten minutes, Tiffaneigh drew to a halt, putting one hand on my upper arm to let me know to stop. When I glanced at her, she put one finger to her lips. Why were we stopping?

Then I realized that I didn't see Professor Ng ahead of us anymore. No sound of crackling branches or footprints ahead. No movement through the trees. No flash of fabric or anything. He'd vanished. The only thing in sight other than trees was the small woodshed beside the path. If this was the same building I'd spotted last weekend, Professor Zimm had been buried roughly twenty feet ahead of us.

Putting my lips next to Tiffaneigh's ear, I whispered what I knew.

She jerked her head toward the shed and pointed, a question in her eyes. Silently, I nodded.

According to the sign on the outer wall, this building was created in the 1800s by volunteers who used it to run a soup kitchen. Seemed like a strange place to serve food, but no one asked me. The room was a small box, containing not much other than an old, coal stove, and a boarded-up window that reminded me of the snack bar at Kevin's high school baseball games.

There weren't any electric lights in the shed, obviously, so we couldn't see much else. I swept the light of my phone around the floor, but there wasn't any place for Professor Ng to hide. We'd lost him.

"Well, darn," Tiffaneigh said beside me. She'd obviously reached the same conclusion. "I guess we should go back."

"Yeah," I said. "Do you want to look at the burial site first? It's right around the corner. Maybe he's there, and we just couldn't see him. They say the murderer always returns to the scene of the crime."

"Sure. In bad movies."

A loud bang rang out. Tiffaneigh screamed like she'd been shot. I jumped out of my skin. Not literally. My phone clattered to the ground and skittered away. Everything went dark.

I whirled around, expecting to see Professor Ng wielding a machete or pointing a gun at us. Instead, the door had slammed shut. A shiver went down my spine. Probably the wind, I told myself, desperate to slow my racing heart.

Shaking my head at my silliness, I moved to open the door. Only one problem. The metal rod serving as a handle didn't move. I tugged, I pushed, I twisted. Nothing happened. The door wouldn't budge.

Tiffaneigh moved up beside me in the darkness. "Here, let me try."

"Be my guest." Maybe she could unlock doors with her mind. She wouldn't appreciate my snide commentary, though, so I watched while she shoved and yanked at the door, twisting a knob on the lever that turned uselessly.

Tiffaneigh and I came to the same realization at the same moment.

Professor Ng had locked us in.

CHAPTER TWENTY-ONE

OKAY, we could manage this. No big deal. Deep breaths.

There were seven noble gases on the periodic table: Helium. Neon. Argon. Krypton. Xenon. Radon. Oganesson.

With a huff, Tiffaneigh pushed away from the door. "It's fine, why don't you stand there while I get help?"

Her words jolted me into action. Right. Call for help. Because this wasn't the 1800s, and we both had phones. Except I'd dropped mine, and without any light, it wouldn't be easy to find. Dropping into a crouch, I ran my fingers over the ground while Tiffaneigh dug in her backpack for her own device. To remain calm, I mentally recited the alkali metals. Sodium. Lithium. Cesium.

There! Finally. My phone.

My elation quickly faded away when the light came on and a message on the front informed me there was no service. Zero bars. Couldn't even text.

"There's no signal," I said. I shouldn't be surprised. When we found Professor Zimm's body, Kevin had to hike to the parking lot to call the police.

"Me, neither." Tiffaneigh sighed. "I guess we're stuck here."

At her confirmation, panic threatened to overwhelm me. As long as we had our phones and the ability to call for help, we were fine. But without that option, doubt started to close in. I barely knew where we were. It would be dark soon. There were no electric lights in the nature preserve for obvious reasons. I wasn't confident I could navigate back to the school's parking lot in the dark without being able to pull up a map on my phone. No one had any reason to wander the preserve in February, so we weren't likely to be rescued.

No one knew I'd come with Tiffaneigh after class. For that matter, no one even knew my class schedule. Kevin would notice if I didn't make it home for dinner, but he'd probably think I was eating at Rusty's. It would never occur to him to look for me in an abandoned building in the middle of the Nature Preserve.

Even if he did, sunset in upstate New York came early in February. It would be dark at least an hour before my brother even left work, and the temperature dropped fast. Tiffaneigh and I would turn into popsicles with nothing but each other to keep warm.

Just when I thought things couldn't get worse, Tiffaneigh pulled a gun out of her backpack.

A hysterical scream escaped me. "I knew it! You killed Professor Zimm because you were worried that the group project was going to ruin your grade."

"Don't be stupid," she said. "If that was it, I'd have killed Brad. You and I would easily get an A without him."

While that shouldn't have comforted me, her words rang true. I'd thought the same thing myself. "So you're planning to shoot the door open?"

"Do you have a better idea?"

"I don't know. Maybe. Let me think." Turning away, I paced the small structure. There wasn't a lot to this shack. The window, boarded up from the outside. An old tub that must've been used to wash dishes back when this place served food. A stove. A couple of old plates in the cupboard. Hmmm.

"Yeah, That's super helpful. Let's climb into the cupboards to get out," Tiffaneigh said, following the direction of my gaze. "When Professor Ng comes back to kill us, I'm telling him to take you first."

"Or you could shoot him, and we could both leave here alive."

"Touché. Can I shoot the lock yet?"

"Hold on. I'm thinking."

Hoping she didn't shoot me in the back for acting weird, I pulled a couple of tin plates and a cup off the shelves. I carried them to the small counter beside the window and mimed putting food on them.

"Great. You've lost it."

"I'm trying to concentrate."

"What are you doing?"

I grasped for an excuse more believable than trying to trigger a vision, which was of course my goal. "This helps me think."

She rolled her eyes and flopped onto one of the chairs.

With several deep breaths, I centered myself, reaching for my powers. In my mind's eye, the plates shone with a silvery glimmer. Not much, but something. I opened my eyes, picked up one, and again pretended to put food on it. Then I turned and walked toward the door, offering both plate and cup to Tiffaneigh.

She vanished.

The air shimmered. People filled the room, sitting at every table. A fire roared on the hearth, filling the room with light and warmth. I worked at the stove, stirring something. Other women walked around, filling plates. They wore hairnets and dresses with long aprons covering them. Not a cell phone or a pair of yoga pants in sight.

I tilted my face to the sky, smiling as sunlight warmed me.

Sunlight inside?

Opening my eyes, I spotted an open in the ceiling, a vent for the smoke from the stovepipe to escape.

And there it was: escape.

When the vision receded, Tiffaneigh was pressed even more firmly against the door than I thought possible, and she clutched the gun as if it were a lifeline. "What just happened?"

I held my hands up. "Don't shoot. I have an idea."

Since no one had been here in a couple dozen decades, dust and other things covered the inside of the roof. But now that I knew what to look for, I clearly saw the square outline above the stove. The old stovepipe still pointed at the spot, but part of it must have rusted away, because it didn't quite touch.

The opening was small. It might be locked. Or it might save us.

Only one way to find out.

Turning away, I climbed up the stove, balancing my weight on the heavy metal that covered each burner. I didn't have any idea how sturdy these things were, but it looked like cast iron. It held.

"Um, Aly?"

"Look." Reaching over my head, I stretched for the roof. I wasn't tall, but thankfully neither were people in the 1800s. My fingers made contact easily. The wood shifted with a creak. A cold wind entered the room. I welcomed it, along with the accompanying sliver of light filtering through the trees.

"Ohhh. How did you know that was there?"

"It was just, um, an inkling I had."

She studied me for a long minute, lips pressed together in a grim line. "Right. Well, come on down."

"Huh?"

"I'm taller than you. It'll be easier for me to climb out. Then I can come around and open the door."

…Or leave me to die. She must've seen the look on my face, because she said, "Look. I've been packing heat all this time. If I wanted to kill you, I had plenty of opportunities."

Her directness truly was oddly refreshing. There was no arguing with that logic, so I simply stepped off the stove, back onto the ground. To my surprise, she flipped the gun around, holding it by the barrel to offer me the handle. "Here. Safety's on."

It was the last thing I expected, but finally, I realized that maybe I could trust Tiffaneigh after all. "Thanks. Good luck."

"I don't need luck," she said. "I was a cheerleader for four years in high school. I've got this."

Of course she was. Before I even finished thinking up an appropriate response, she was out the hole, and I heard her feet moving across the roof. I'd just finished tucking the gun back in her bag when a metal screech filled the shed. The door swung open.

"Good teamwork!" she said. "Now, let's get out of here before he comes back. Once we're safe, you can tell me the truth."

As suspected, darkness had started to fall while we were trapped. A chill washed over me, highlighting the need to move quickly. It would be pitch dark soon. Our cell phone flashlights weren't terrible, but they didn't penetrate the thick February darkness as much as I would have liked. With every step, I thought about the things lurking in the darkness. Coyotes. Murderers.

M. Mendelevium. Magnesium. Moscovi—

"What are you talking about?"

Until Tiffaneigh interrupted me, I hadn't realized I'd been speaking out loud. Good thing the darkness hid my face; it was probably purple with mortification. "Um…when I get nervous, I like to recite the elements of the periodic table."

"Oh." She paused. "You should start at the beginning, then. Element one is hydrogen."

"Two is helium," I replied.

"Lithium."

She reached over, taking my hand in hers. Finally, I started to feel better. We continued our game, repeating the elements back and forth as we wandered down the path. Around the time we got to element forty-seven, silver, I felt comfortable enough to tell her the truth about how I found the body. The whole truth, including how I knew that button belonged to the killer and I'd used my psychic abilities to get us out of the locked shed.

When I finished, she was quiet for a long time. "Why go with me into the woods if you can just use your powers to find out who the killer is?"

"I can't," I said ruefully. "I know someone who could get a reading on the button, but police took it into evidence. I can't ask for it back. Without that, I'd need the murder weapon or something with Professor Zimm when she died, and I haven't found anything yet."

"Hmmm."

We walked in silence, lost in our thoughts until the electric lights that meant we'd found the edge of campus came into view.

A shout of joy escaped me.

Ten feet further down the path, I stopped dead in my tracks. I must be hallucinating from the stress, because I could've sworn I saw someone walking toward us. The person whose face always brought me joy. The sight of him filled me with happiness.

"Sam! What are you doing here?"

"I, uh..." His face turned red. "I came to rescue you."

"Awww, That's sweet. I rescued myself. Well, Tiffaneigh and I did it together."

"I can see that. Are you okay?"

"I'm fine, too!" Tiffaneigh said loudly. "Thanks for asking."

Quickly, I introduced them as we walked to my car. When we got there, I pointedly told Tiffaneigh I'd talk to her later. She got the hint. "I'll see you at the police station, then? We have to report this as soon as possible. Professor Ng is still on the loose."

Darn it, I'd almost forgotten all about him when Sam appeared, but she was right.

"Absolutely! Give me ten minutes." I turned my attention back to Sam. "Don't think I'm not happy to see you, but— what are you doing here?"

"I went by your house after I closed the store, and Kyle said you hadn't been home yet. Since we had plans for this evening. I was worried. Mrs. Patel said that you're usually home by four on Tuesdays and Thursdays." He paused. "You're shaking. It's freezing. Let's talk about this in the car."

He didn't even finish his suggestion before I'd slid behind the wheel of my Prius and hit the ignition switch, unlocking the passenger door to let him join me. A quick scan of the parking lot while I waited for Sam to walk around the car showed that Professor Ng's RAV4 had disappeared.

After settling into the seat, he said, "Okay, so you just decided to go for a hike in the freezing cold?"

"Tiffaneigh ambushed me after class. No one knew where I was."

"Kyle knew."

I blinked at him repeatedly. "Excuse me?"

"I can't explain it, exactly," Sam said. "I said I was worried. He walked over and hugged me. Then he told me exactly where to find you. If he were older, he probably could've drawn a map."

Impressive. I should've been surprised, but I'd had my

suspicions for a while now. The whole thing with Kyle finding Professor Zimm's glasses seemed weird, but at the time, I'd shrugged it off as a coincidence. Between that and the scene I'd witnessed in the mirror, I was more surprised I hadn't guessed what form his powers took.

"Not to sound rude, but I'm a little surprised you'd risk hypothermia on the word of a three-year-old." I smiled at him. "Thank you."

His eyes met mine, and one hand came up to cup my cheek. "I'd risk anything for you."

Before I could talk myself out of it, I launched my lips at his face. In retrospect, it was probably the least smooth first kiss ever. Due to an unfortunate miscalculation, my lips started somewhere around his nose. But he quickly guided my face where it needed to go.

There. That was nice.

"I've wanted to do that for a long time," he admitted when we pulled apart.

"Me, too." I sighed. "I'd like to do a lot more of it, preferably somewhere less public. But Tiffaneigh and I were just locked in a wood cabin and left for dead, so I need to get to the police station."

"Did you see who did it?"

"No, but we were following Professor Ng. He was wandering the woods, and he had a shovel. Right after we lost him, the shed door slammed shut." I paused. "I don't know where he went. Was probably digging our graves when we escaped."

Sam shivered. "I'm glad you got out on your own. I was terrified I'd be too late."

"It means a lot that you came." I kissed him again. "I hate to say this, but you probably shouldn't come to the police station with me. People will ask too many questions."

He nodded regretfully. After one more peck on my mouth, he pulled away. "I'm going to follow you, though, to make sure you get there okay. Don't argue. We don't know where Professor Ng went."

The thought of Sam Green caring enough to follow me anywhere to check up on my well-being sent a thrill through me. Arguing was the last thing on my mind.

When I arrived at the police station, Tiffaneigh's car was already in the lot. Through the large front window, I saw her sitting on the wooden chair beside Doug's desk. He typed furiously while she spoke, nodding along. To my surprise, Sheriff Matthews wasn't in sight, and the door to his office was closed. On most of my trips to the police station, the door was open whenever the Sheriff went out. I wondered who he was talking to in there. Seemed to me he'd be interested in solving Professor Zimm's murder, so why was Doug the only one out here talking to Tiffaneigh?

Bracing myself against the cold, I opened the car door and raced for the inside.

"It's about time you got here!" Tiffaneigh snapped. "Were you sitting in the parking lot making out with that hottie while I did all the work?"

My face grew warm.

"Hottie?" Doug asked.

"That's not relevant," I said. "As Tiffaneigh has probably told you, Professor Ng killed Professor Zimm, and he just tried to kill us."

Doug's expression didn't change. Either I'd just repeated a bunch of information he already knew, or he'd make a terrific poker player. I looked from him to Tiffaneigh and back. "I just spoke, right? You're both looking at me like maybe it was only in my head."

Tiffaneigh nodded.

Doug snorted. "I heard you. I'm just confused." He raised his voice. "Sheriff? Can you come out here, please?"

The door to Sheriff Matthews's office opened, and he filled the doorway. He was a tall, sturdy black man, with short, greying hair and an unfortunate willingness to do the mayor's bidding. One reason that we didn't get along.

Another man stepped into the main room behind the sheriff, and my jaw dropped. Before I could say a word, the newcomer let out a yell and pointed at me and Tiffaneigh. "There they are! The two girls who tried to kill me."

CHAPTER TWENTY-TWO

AT PROFESSOR NG'S PROCLAMATION, chaos broke out. Tiffaneigh dove under Doug's desk, pulling the coat from the back of his chair over her as if it were bulletproof. He protested loudly, trying to talk to his uncle at the same time. Professor Ng shot back into Sheriff Matthews's office and slammed the door.

Meanwhile, I stood in the midst of it all thinking that psychic powers would be more useful if they helped me avoid situations like this one. Professor Ng thought Tiffaneigh and I wanted to kill him? If he'd been trying to kill us, it didn't make sense for him to come straight to the police station and report what happened. He didn't know Tiffaneigh was armed.

My conversation with Ethan came back to me. He'd been shocked to hear me suggest Professor Ng might have killed his wife. Swore up and down they were old friends, and Professor Ng was a pacifist. I hadn't gotten a chance to google the election thing yet, but that wasn't the type of story a person made up. There was no reason for Ethan to protect Professor Ng—he'd been genuinely shocked and distressed to learn about his wife's death.

Sure, people changed. From pacifist to murderer? I supposed Professor Ng could have been lying to get votes. Wouldn't be the first time. But the more I thought about it, the more it seemed Tiffaneigh had gotten something wrong.

After a moment, I put two fingers in my mouth and let out the piercing whistle Kevin taught me when we were kids, before he left for college.

Mom never forgave him for that. She made me promise to teach it to Kyle as soon as possible after moving in with them. Which wasn't in my best interests, so hard pass.

Silence descended as everyone turned to stare at me. Sheriff Matthews put his hands on his hips. "Aly Reynolds. I should've known."

I raised my hands. "I'm just here to report a crime."

Tiffaneigh crawled out from behind Doug's desk, taking a moment to smooth her clothes and replace his coat. "This seems like a good time to mention the gun in my bag."

"What? You didn't leave it in the car?" I asked her.

She shrugged as Doug rushed between us and grabbed her backpack from the counter. "It's legally purchased, licensed, and registered in my name."

"Do you have a concealed carry permit?" Doug asked as he fished it out.

"Well…" Her face turned red. "I've been planning to apply for one, but then someone killed my professor and I needed it for protection."

The door to the Sheriff's office opened a crack, and a sliver of Professor Ng's face appeared. "What are you doing? Arrest them!"

The sheriff's eyes traveled from his doorway to me to Tiffaneigh, to the gun Doug now held with a white handkerchief he'd found somewhere. "Why don't we all sit down together and figure this out? Is anyone else armed?"

"I am," Doug offered.

"Lucky you," Sheriff Matthews said. "Bag and tag that

girl's gun, put it in evidence, and join us when you're done, okay? We'll need to run a forensics report."

Turning, he led me and Tiffaneigh into a small, windowless room holding nothing but a cheap wooden table and two folding chairs. A large mirror on the wall told me this must be the interrogation room. He directed me and Tiffaneigh to sit, then disappeared, leaving the door open.

"What's going on?" I asked. "Are we under arrest?"

"No one is under arrest," Sheriff Matthews said from the doorway. He ushered Professor Ng into the room, produced another chair from somewhere outside the door, and pointed for him to sit across from us. Sheriff Matthews remained standing by the door.

"Girls, Professor Ng came to me tonight to report that the two of you followed him through the woods. When it became clear that you weren't merely headed in the same direction, he began to fear for his safety. He started walking faster, and so did you."

"We were trying to prove he killed Professor Zimm," Tiffaneigh said. "I saw him lurking around the nature preserve, acting suspicious. He even had a shovel."

"Yeah, and then he locked us up so we would freeze to death," I added.

"You were going to kill me!" Professor Ng burst out.

"We were not," Tiffaneigh said.

"What were you doing in the nature preserve so close to dark?" I asked, desperate to get back on track.

He pulled himself up to his full height and lifted his nose. "I am the resident director of botany. I work on several areas in the preserve, including some plants that needed to be relocated."

Oh, right. He was doing plant things. My cheeks grew warm as I started to realize the magnitude of our mistake. "Hold on. Then why did you lock us up?"

"I got scared to see two girls following me. You were

never in any danger—I came here so police could go let you out right away. Then you act like I'm overreacting when you admit following me while carrying a gun the whole time."

"Ms. Pratt? What do you have to say for yourself?"

"My dad bought that gun for my birthday," she said. "You don't go tracking a killer through the woods unarmed."

"You're the killer!" Professor Ng burst out.

"Everyone, stop." Sheriff Matthews's command cut through the outburst. "This seems to be a simple misunderstanding. We all want to know who killed Tabitha Zimm. You're all concerned by the idea of a killer on campus, I understand that. Ms. Pratt, where were you the night of February fifth?"

Her cheeks turned pink. "I was at home, studying."

She was lying, but since I knew she hadn't killed Professor Zimm, there was no point in calling her out. I couldn't explain how I knew, and ballistics should prove the bullet didn't match her gun.

"Did anyone see you?" Doug asked.

"I don't think so. My dad was working. He's Willow Falls PD, you know. I believe he helped you with your last murder investigation."

"Yes, You've reminded me six times in the past fifteen minutes."

"Just want to make sure all the facts are straight," she said sweetly. "Can I use the bathroom?"

"Right that way," he said wearily before turning to me. "Aly?"

"I worked at Missing Pieces all day. Olive was away, but Sam came in to help out. He was in and out. After we closed at six, I went home to have dinner with Kevin and Kyle."

"What about after dinner?"

"I was watching Hallmark movies on my iPad. Kevin should be able to confirm I never left the house."

He scratched a note on the pad in front of him. "Professor Ng? Let's hear it."

"Teaching my Women in Environmental Biology advanced seminar to fifteen graduate students, as I do every Friday night in the spring," he said smugly. "I can get you the names and contact information for everyone enrolled."

My face fell with disappointment. Not that I wanted Professor Ng to be a murderer, but this confirmed I was completely on the wrong track. I thought I might actually find the killer using science and logic. With Olive out of commission and Doug not likely to give me the button, there seemed to be no hope of solving the crime any other way.

"It sounds like this was all a big misunderstanding," Sheriff Matthews said. "Professor, next time you think someone is following you, consider running away and calling 911. Girls, leave the detective work to the professionals. For now, you can go."

I started to leave, but something stopped me. "Professor, why did you think Tiffaneigh and I wanted to kill you? Because we were walking in the woods?"

"Of course not. You make me sound paranoid," he snapped. "I thought you were going to kill me because I saw you nosing around Professor Zimm's office after she died."

My cheeks grew warm.

"You broke into her office?" Doug asked.

"No!" I said. "Her husband asked me to pick up a few personal items."

As I finished explaining, Tiffaneigh reappeared. She stood quietly in the doorway for a minute, listening.

"What about your friend here hounding everyone about her grade and extra credit?" Professor Ng asked. "The two of you have been everywhere this week."

"It's not a crime to want to do well in school!" Tiffaneigh said loudly.

"No, but it is a crime to stalk a professor," he replied.

"She's been stalking you?" I asked.

Sheriff Matthews put one hand on my arm. "Excuse me, Ms. Reynolds, but I think I can handle this."

It was on the tip of my tongue to point out that he hadn't figured out much yet, but I strongly preferred to stay in the police department's good graces. Or at least no further away than usual. Especially until I got that button back.

"Tiffaneigh, Aly, I think we have all we need from you," Doug said. "Thanks for coming by."

"I wasn't stalking anyone!" Tiffaneigh said.

"And I'm not nosing around," I said. "I'm trying to find a murderer!"

Sheriff Matthews cleared his throat loudly. "Enough! Professor, why don't you accompany me back to my office? I'd like to get some more information. Girls, you're free to go."

The words sounded like a request, but since Doug took me and Tiffaneigh each by an elbow and escorted us through the front door, it seemed clear we'd officially worn out our welcome.

One other thing seemed clear: Professor Ng could be removed from my suspect list. No way he snuck into the preserve and killed Professor Zimm in the middle of teaching a class.

So who killed Professor Zimm? Tiffaneigh seemed to care enough about her grade to kill, but she had a solid alibi. So did Brad and Ethan.

When we got outside, Tiffaneigh turned to me. "Thanks for coming with me. Sorry about getting you locked in a cabin and nearly murdered."

"You weren't nearly murdered," Doug cut in. "Professor Ng never had any intention of hurting anyone."

"It's okay," I said, ignoring him. "Thanks for keeping me calm."

"No problem." She grinned and looked at the time on her phone. "I gotta go. Study group."

From the pink touching her cheeks, I suspected what she had was less a "study group" and more a "secret rendezvous with Brad." But it was none of my business, so I just told her I'd see her in class next week.

She paused. "Oh, hey. I've still got that box in my trunk. Come with me?"

Her eyes widened so comically I was glad Doug looked at me instead of her. It was painfully obvious she wanted to tell me something privately. "Sure. See you later, Doug."

We walked behind her car, where Tiffaneigh popped the trunk and leaned inside, way over the box. Then she reached into the pocket of her sweater.

"What are you doing?"

"I've got something for you."

When she pulled her hand out and opened it, my jaw dropped open. "You stole the button?"

"Stole, borrowed. Po-tah-to, po-tay-to."

"You can't take that! It's evidence."

"Look, they'll never know it's gone," she said. "I swapped it with one from Doug's coat."

So that was why she spent so much time under the desk when Professor Ng appeared. "I could kiss you right now."

"I'd prefer you didn't. Just take the button, and make sure you get it back after we find the killer."

I grabbed the button and shoved it into my pocket, then swept Tiffaneigh up in a hug and spun her around. I didn't even care if Doug or the Sheriff were looking outside.

"Put me down!"

"Sorry, I got a little carried away," I said. "I gotta go."

With a squeal, I raced toward my car. I needed to get to Olive! As soon as I slid into the driver's seat, I texted her to let her know what happened.

My high spirits deflated a moment later when I remembered: Olive lost her powers. Until we figured out how to bring them back, she couldn't help.

The button was useless.

CHAPTER TWENTY-THREE

SINCE RUSHING OVER to see Olive wasn't going to help, I decided to pay Mary a visit before going home. She'd been dodging my calls, texts, email, and FaceTime requests ever since Olive passed out, and it was time to get answers.

For the entire drive, I practiced what to say once I arrived. Based on my conversation with Amira, I strongly suspected Mary had been the one to put the spell on the rocking horse. But why? Was she so sure Kevin killed her sister that she'd want to hurt me or Kyle? How did the spell even work—it didn't affect me at all. What did she have against Kyle?

My nephew had powers, definitely. It seemed to run in the family on both sides. Was Mary the one in the mirror, trying to use Kyle's powers for some reason? That didn't quite fit, since she seemed convinced Kevin killed her sister, but she could also be a good liar. I supposed blaming someone else for your crimes was a good way to deflect suspicion.

That last thought made me shiver and wish I'd asked Tiffaneigh to come along for protection. Or Rusty, who would be much more effective now that Tiffaneigh's gun was being tested for residue by the police department.

When I arrived at Mary's house, everything was dark. It

occurred to me that I didn't know what she did for a living. She could be at work still or out with friends. It felt like midnight after the day I'd had, but it was barely dinner time. My stomach howled at the thought of food.

After running to Mr. Patel's restaurant for takeout, I returned to Mary's house and waited while I ate. Still no lights, no car. No sign of life. For several minutes, the delicious chicken saag and samosas made everything better. Then I realized that my gas needle was dangerously low. It was too cold to sit in the car without the engine running, so Mary would have to forgive me for waiting inside. It's not breaking and entering when you're family, right?

The front door was locked, so I wandered around to the back. Unlike where I grew up, this area didn't have a lot of fences. More likely to be seen, sure, but fewer obstacles. The back door slid open easily at my touch. Excellent.

Inside, the air carried a bite. Mary either wasn't coming home for a couple of hours or didn't have her heater on an automatic timer. I found the thermostat easily enough, but it required a four-digit code to make any changes. Oh, well. Mary must have blankets, and my coat wasn't bad. Too bad I couldn't conjure a vision of a nice, warm stay on the beach.

Hmmm. Could I?

Using the flashlight on my phone, I moved around the house, looking for some item that might give me summery visions. After a moment, though, I realized that it was pointless. I couldn't see nearly enough. With my car sitting outside, it made no sense to wander around in the dark, walking into stuff. Mary would know I was here as soon as she pulled into the driveway, so I might as well use the lights. Even though she'd been avoiding me, I didn't think she would skip coming inside just so she didn't have to talk to me.

What would trigger a vision of warmer places? Sandals, probably, but I did not want to wear Mary's shoes. Sunglasses? Sunblock? Since I needed to start somewhere, I wandered into the small bathroom off the living room. Just a sink and toilet, no cupboard or shelves. Nothing sitting on the counter except a bottle of hand soap. There must be another bathroom.

Inside the larger of the bedrooms, I flipped the overhead switch. The room was pristine. Nothing on top of the dresser. No clutter on the nightstands. Perfectly made bed. Something felt wrong. Moving into the bathroom, I opened the medicine cabinet to find it empty. So was the cupboard.

No shampoo in the shower.

The bad feeling in my gut was growing. Rushing to the closet, I threw the double doors open. Not a single piece of clothing in sight.

A slam reverberated through the house. I jumped.

"Hello?" A man's voice. Not Mary. What was going on? I supposed she could have a boyfriend, but the lack of personal items in the house was dragging me toward the inescapable conclusion that she had skipped town. "Who's there?"

"Hello? I'm looking for my…sister-in-law." Is the sister of your sister-in-law also an in-law? Sister-in-law once removed? Friend? Nope, definitely not a friend.

The man in the doorway looked familiar, but I couldn't quite place him. He had shiny, perfectly parted blond hair and huge gums. "How did you get in here? Where's my sign and lockbox?"

I blinked at him. "I'm sorry? I came to visit my sister-in-law, but she's not home."

He laughed bitterly. "Not home? No one has lived here for over a year."

"Oh, no," I said. "I get why you would think that. She was in rehab for a bit, but then she came back. This is her house."

"This is my house," he said. "Well, my client's."

My phone rang. I silenced it without looking at the screen, trying to process what this guy was saying. For a long moment, I stared at him. Sign, lockbox. Client. "You're a realtor?"

"Bingo! Todd Lacroix, at your service."

At least that explained why he looked familiar. His picture was on every bus stop bench in Shady Grove. All four of them. "Aly Reynolds. I'm sorry, my sister-in-law gave me this address and said she lived here."

"Looks like she was playing a joke on you. Sending you on a wild goose chase," he said. "Sorry, but I'm going to have to ask you to leave. And get an alarm, I guess. Thank goodness the neighbor called me when they saw someone lurking in the bushes outside."

Hmmph. I didn't lurk.

After apologizing about seventeen more times, I left. As soon as the car door shut behind me, I turned on the heater and rubbed my hands together to generate warmth. I still didn't know if I could conjure a vision of warmth and sun. Things to worry about later. For now, I picked up my phone to see who called.

Kevin. The one and only person whose calls I nearly always answered. If he needed help with Kyle, I wanted to know about it immediately. I called him back. "Hey, what's up?"

"I just read your text. You said you went to visit Mary?"

"Uh, yeah. I hope that's okay." I was about to launch into the story of how her house was now empty and she never lived there and she might be a witch when he spoke.

"It's fine with me," he said. "She's been through a lot, and family can help. I just didn't realize she was allowed to have visitors."

"What?"

"I told you, she's in rehab. Isn't that where you are?"

"No, I'm…" At the address she gave me. The empty house. Where she gave me a booby-trapped child's toy before skipping town. "You're sure she's still at the facility?"

"Positive. I spoke with her nurse ten minutes ago. Aren't you there?"

His words hit me like a thunderbolt. I could barely think well enough to answer his question. "No. I stopped for dinner before realizing I didn't have the address. Then I saw you called."

"I've got it. Do you need a pen?"

I needed a lot of things at the moment. Mary was in rehab this whole time. Who had I met, and what did they have to do with any of this?

While I was rummaging in my backpack to write down the real address—with no idea whether I actually wanted to go there—my phone beeped again. This time it was a text from Olive.

Bring me the button. My powers are back.

The timing should have surprised me, but if Olive had been attacked by a spell, maybe it faded once the person who cast it got a certain distance away. That would certainly support my "Mary skipped town theory." Or NotMary. Whoever it was.

"Kevin, I'm sorry, I've got to go. I'll be home soon."

Before he could respond, I hung up and set my GPS for Missing Pieces.

Even though Olive's message had told me she was fine, a huge smile split my face in two when I arrived at Missing Pieces to find Olive back in place behind the counter where she belonged. I'd been so afraid that she'd never get her powers back, and it would be my fault.

My tackle hug nearly knocked her off her feet. "Thank goodness you're okay! I've been so worried."

"You? What about me, having to hear from my son that you almost got yourself killed in the woods?"

I averted my eyes. "I guess it was too much to hope he wouldn't mention it."

"Yes." She laughed. "I'll lecture you later. Where's the button?"

I produced it triumphantly. "Just don't ask how I got it."

"Oh, dear. Hush and let me focus." Olive took the button and shook it out of the bag. Her palm closed around it, and her eyes fluttered shut. "I see a boy. Probably about your age."

This style of coat was everywhere on campus, so not shocking. Anyone who wasn't rocking L.L. Bean wore it.

"He's tall, athletic. Looks like he exercises, but he's not overly muscular. Maybe a runner?"

My mind raced, but it wasn't enough. She could be talking about half the male student body. "Can you see his face?"

"There he is! Blond hair, blue eyes. Wearing a Maloney College hat. Hold on. There's something else."

I waited patiently. Olive's visions didn't come with a name tag. She hadn't known my name when I first came in. But she'd see as much as she could, and it could all be useful.

"A jersey. He does play sports. Basketball. Looks like number fifty-four."

My breath caught in my throat.

Element fifty-four was xenon. A dense noble gas found in the Earth's atmosphere. Didn't help. I still couldn't breathe.

Olive opened her eyes. "What's wrong? Do you know him?"

"He's in my class," I choked out. "Number fifty-four is Brad Stevens."

The BS meeting. It wasn't code for a waste of time, like I'd thought. It was literally a meeting with Brad Stevens. Who had been with Tiffaneigh when Professor Zimm died. Was the timing off? Maybe she'd died earlier than I'd thought? Brad could have killed her, dropped her in the preserve, then run into Tiffaneigh after cleaning up Professor Zimm's office.

Olive's powers had never been wrong. I missed something.

Brad and Tiffaneigh were together that night.

Tiffaneigh hadn't done it.

But they were together now.

"What's wrong?" Olive asked. "I thought you'd be excited to find out who the killer is."

"Tiffaneigh." The words stuck in my throat. "She's at Brad's house right now, and Doug took her gun. I have to go."

CHAPTER TWENTY-FOUR

MY MIND REELED as I scrambled for my coat and gloves. I needed to get to Brad's as soon as possible, make sure my friend was okay.

"Hold on there, Aly," Olive said. "You can't confront him yourself. You'll get killed."

"If I don't go, I'll get Tiffaneigh killed."

"Call the police," she insisted. "Or Tiffaneigh. Tell her to run."

If they were doing what I suspected, she wasn't going to stop to answer the phone. I needed to go over there and get her out.

"There's no time!" I was already halfway to the door. "Call them, tell them what you saw. Tiffaneigh helped me earlier. I need to help her now."

"Can't you text?"

Duh.

"Yes, yes, I can. If she responds, I'll turn around and head straight home. Meanwhile, I can text while I walk to my car."

"Okay, but I'm sending the police to Brad's house."

My used Prius went faster than I thought possible as I raced toward 27 Maple Street. Mentally, I cursed myself for dismissing Brad as a suspect so easily. He just didn't seem like a guy who cared enough about anything to kill over it. Then I had the vision and saw him with Tiffaneigh. I should've dug deeper, especially after I saw that email about the meeting. I just saw "BS" and went with the most common usage, especially since I'd thought Brad had been cleared by my vision. Stupid lack of timestamps.

To my surprise, Tiffaneigh's car was pulling up when I arrived. If she'd driven here straight from the police station, she should have been here at least half an hour ago. Then the interior lights came on, and I realized she must've gone home and showered. Her dark hair shone, unbraided for a change and hanging in loose waves down her back. She wore makeup and probably didn't smell like the inside of a musty old shack.

Great idea. Wish I'd thought of it.

When she saw me approach, her eyes widened. She cracked her window just enough to talk without letting too much heat out. "What are you doing here? Don't tell me you ditched that hot guy back at the preserve for Brad. Because if you want to trade—"

I held up one hand. "I beg you to stop talking. I'm here to save you. Brad killed Professor Zimm. Let's go. We need to call the police."

"What are you talking about?"

I hesitated, but if I wanted her to leave with me instead of going inside, I needed to be at least partially honest. After this afternoon, I could trust her. "The button I found belongs to Brad."

"Your friend read it?"

"She did, and she described Brad perfectly. Even saw the number on his jersey."

"Okay, I trust you." Relief flooded through me until she swung the door open. "Let's go find the coat."

"What? No! Let's leave."

"Don't be silly. You've got a lost mass-produced button stolen from the crime scene. That's not enough to get a warrant. We'll get laughed out of the police station if we're not arrested. If we find the coat, that helps. Come on."

"Don't we need a warrant?'

"No. We're not police, and they didn't ask us to come here."

They had not. I shifted from one foot to the other. "This isn't a good idea. Hold on, I'll call Doug."

Before I even found my phone in my bag, Tiffaneigh made it halfway to the front porch. With a groan of frustration, I followed. I grabbed her hand, but the door swung open before I could drag her back toward the street.

Lacey stood inside the doorway, looking like a model for Prada. Not that I knew what Prada looked like, but she was all fancy with a lot of makeup and glamorous hair. She beamed at the sight of us. "Girls! Welcome back. What can I do for you?"

"Hi! Sorry to bother you," I said brightly. "We're looking for Brad. Is he here?"

"Come in, come in! I'll get him."

The last time I'd been here, we'd spread out our books and stuff on the massive table in the kitchen. This time, Lacey took us to a small room off the foyer. I'd never thought people still had formal sitting rooms, but this room looked exactly like I would've imagined a nineteenth-century parlor. Straight-backed chairs with expensive-looking fabric and carved wooden frames, a large fireplace dominating one wall, and a full-length sterling silver mirror standing in the corner.

"Would you like anything to drink?" Lacey asked. "Glass of wine?"

"No, thank you," I said. "We won't be staying long."

"In that case, it was nice to see you again. I'm headed to an exhibit in Albany. I'll tell Brad you're here."

"You could stay with us!" Tiffaneigh burst out. Now that

we were inside the house, she seemed to realize she should have listened to me. Too little, too late.

Lacey laughed. "I appreciate it, but you don't want Brad's mom hanging around. I'll see you later."

"This is a terrible idea," I hissed to Tiffaneigh as the door closed behind Brad's mom. "We're supposed to be getting away from him, not hanging out with the fam."

"All of a sudden, my stomach hurts. I can't believe I came here without my gun."

"I still can't believe you pulled a gun on me. Or that I would voluntarily hang out with you after."

"I'm an acquired taste. Give it time. You'll love me."

A flash of her reaching out to take my hand in the woods while reciting the elements of the periodic table came back to me. "Love might be a strong word, but you are growing on me. Like a fungus."

"I'm serious!" she said. "Anyway, listen. My dad told me the Shady Grove PD still hasn't found the gun that killed Professor Zimm. It could be in this house. Let's find it before Brad gets here."

"The eighteen seconds before Brad comes in to catch us going through his stuff? If you're serious, for your sake, I hope you can outrun me."

"Very funny," she said out the side of her mouth. "But I ran track in high school, so I'll let it go."

Of course she did.

"Check this out," Tiffaneigh said, going straight toward the giant mirror in the corner. "Mirror, mirror on the wall, who is the fairest of them all?"

I laughed, lowering my voice. "You, my dear, are the fairest of them all."

"Shh! Don't let the evil queen hear you say that."

The two of us doubled over, the stress making everything ten times funnier than it actually was. When we recovered, I looked around for a clock. It shouldn't have taken long for Lacey to tell Brad we were here, so where was he?

"Here, you try."

"You're just going to tell me you're the pretty one, aren't you?"

She fluffed her hair and sniffed. "You'll have to wait and see."

Since we had nothing better to do, I decided to play along. I walked over to the mirror and pulled myself to my full height, smoothing my hands over my hair the way I imagined a bored housewife might. "Mirror, mirror, on the wall."

Then I stopped, my eyes running along the smooth glass. What might this mirror have to tell me? Could I get a glimpse of Brad with Professor Zimm? Taking a deep breath, I tried to unfocus my eyes.

Nothing happened. I was too tense. I started to get annoyed, but told myself to calm down. Katrina's mirror hadn't shown me anything at first, either. I may not have candles or anything here to help with scrying, but there was one thing I always had: me.

"What are you doing?" Tiffaneigh said. "You have to ask the question."

"Shhh. Give me a second."

I centered myself on the frame, gazed into the glass, then closed my eyes. Mentally, I recited the first twenty elements, then opened them. Slowly, I let everything fade out of focus while deep breathing. Something stirred within me. I reached for it. The images in the mirror wavered.

My reflection faded from the glass.

An image swam before my eyes. A pair of haunted blue eyes looked out at me. Red-rimmed, opened so wide the white nearly blinded me. Eyes framed by long, golden lashes. Brad's eyes. A patrician nose, perfectly smooth forehead, lips that normally stretched into a smile. Now, they turned downward in a grimace.

Dirt caked my hands. No longer perfectly-manicured hands.

Three jagged nails sat at the ends of my fingers, as if proclaiming what I'd done. I wore a black overcoat, hanging awkwardly off my frame. It gaped open where one button had disappeared.

Olive had been right. The button did come from Brad's coat. He just wasn't the one wearing it. Because someone else had a very similar coat, and I already knew the two got mixed up.

Everything slid into place. Brad wasn't the person in my vision. The BS meeting. It *was* about Brad, it just wasn't *with* him.

Lacey's pale face glared at me out of the mirror.

A GASP ESCAPED me before I could stop it.

"What's happening?" Tiffaneigh said. "What do you see?"

"I don't understand," I said. "Why would Brad's mother kill Professor Zimm?"

Brad's voice answered from the doorway. "Mom hated Professor Zimm. She couldn't believe she'd failed me, even after Mom offered to make a sizable donation to the science department. Didn't matter that I never did the work. She refused to accept no for an answer."

The sight of him made me jump. Eyes wide, hair disheveled. Looking, to be perfectly honest, quite a bit like the vision I'd had of his mother after she'd committed the murder. In his hand, he held a pistol. I was no gun expert, but it looked like the same one Lacey held in the image across from me. Which had vanished from the mirror.

This couldn't be happening. At twenty-one, I was too young to have so many brushes with death.

Element twenty-one was scandium. Element twenty-two was titanium. Tiffaneigh was twenty-two. Too young to die. We needed to get out of here.

"Brad? What are you talking about?" Tiffaneigh's

voice was calm, so soothing I wondered if she'd had practice at this sort of thing. "No one did anything wrong. Aly and I are going to go so you can rest. You look ill."

"I am sick." He walked into the room and flopped down on the couch. "My mother killed my teacher!"

"We don't know she did it," Tiffaneigh said. "The police are investigating."

My first inclination was to note out the evidence clearly pointed in that direction, but for once, I wisely held my tongue. She shot me a look, as if she heard my thoughts.

"But even if she did," I said, "it's okay. We know you didn't do anything wrong."

"You should blame me." He laughed hollowly. "It's all my fault. You know the real reason I failed?"

Tiffaneigh and I exchanged a look. Finally, I said, "You told us that she had an unfair attendance policy."

Luckily, Brad spoke again. "I refused to go to class. Professor Zimm had a clear attendance policy, but I didn't want to get up at eight a.m., so I never went. Stayed out drinking instead. Now a woman is dead because I didn't want to adult."

I sat on the cushion to his left. Probably I should inch toward the front door instead, but not until we disarmed him. Brad was so upset, he seemed more likely to harm himself than anyone else. I couldn't let him.

A voice in my head strongly suggested I run for the front door, then dial 911. It sounded a lot like Olive. Alas, too late now.

"You couldn't have known what would happen," I said.

"I never believed she would fail me."

"Even if you did, there's no reason to think your mom would kill her because of it."

"Isn't there?" he said. "This is the woman who paid someone to take my SATs. She threatened the other guy who liked the girl I wanted to take to prom. Who knows what she's capable of?"

"You certainly don't." For the second time in less than five minutes, a voice from the doorway made me jump. "Bradley, darling, don't you think it's time you stopped talking?"

All three of us turned in slow motion, despite knowing who we would find. It was bad enough that Tiffaneigh and I had been discovered talking about Lacey by her son. He obviously had an incentive to stop us from leaving, but also—did killing run in the family? We might have been able to talk Brad into letting us go.

On the other hand, Lacey killed a woman over a failing grade and the need to repeat a class. What would she do to keep us from turning her in? No one wanted to exchange a lifetime of alimony and a mini-mansion for an orange jumpsuit.

"Mom! What are you doing home so early?"

Lacey stepped into the room and closed the French doors behind her, turning a key I hadn't noticed earlier in the lock. I swallowed and instinctively moved closer to Brad, which was silly because he clutched a gun in his right hand.

"I was on my way to the art exhibition, and I turned around because your father's second wife is going to be there, and I wanted to change to some flashier jewelry. Something to remind her that even if she got him, I won. It's a good thing I did, or I wouldn't have overheard your conversation." Her voice got higher with every word. "But what I don't understand, Brad, is why you'd be telling your friends such strange stories about me."

Brad's voice was strangely level. "It's not a story, Mom. It's true."

I laughed loudly. "Brad is such a kidder! He almost got us, didn't he, Tiffaneigh?"

On the other side of Brad, Tiffaneigh shot me a grateful look before she immediately picked up my thread. "What a joker! Yeah. What kind of dummies does he think we are? Listen, we should be going. Aly has to babysit her nephew tonight, don't you, Aly?"

At first I thought it was weird that she kept repeating my name, but then I realized she was trying to constantly remind Lacey and Brad that I was a person with a family and feelings, not a threat to their perfect existence.

"Right! You have such a great memory, Tiffaneigh. I promised Kyle we'd have a movie pajama party in the living room. We're setting up a tent and everything."

"That's adorable," Lacey said with a tsk. "I'm afraid you're not going to make it. Neither of you will."

"Why are you standing in front of the door?" Brad asked.

"Obviously, we can't let your friends leave, can we? They know too much."

"We don't know anything," Tiffaneigh said quickly.

Lacey ignored her. "What I can't figure out, though, is how you realized it was me. I covered my tracks. Cleaned up the blood in the office, got my car detailed, used meat to lure animals to the scene. I replaced Brad's missing button so no one would look too closely at his coat."

"I knew because I know how much you care about me, Mom."

"I do care. You're my whole world. I thought I was yours, which is why I'm so surprised by this conversation. You wouldn't betray your darling mother, would you, sweetie?"

Beside me, Brad still clenched the gun in white knuckles. Lacey hadn't budged from her spot in front of the doors, and until she did, Tiffaneigh and I were stuck. My phone was... Yes! My phone was in the fabulous side pocket of my leggings!

An exciting fact, until I realized that the only way to get my hand into my pocket was to run it down the outside of Brad's thigh, since we sat so close on the couch. I also doubted Lacey would stand and watch while I dialed 911.

So much for that plan.

Brad turned to me. "How did you know?"

"What?"

"You and Tiffaneigh figured out my mom killed Professor Zimm. I heard that part. It all made sense when I heard you talking, but I didn't hear how you knew."

I laughed nervously. "I don't know what you're talking about. Professor Ng killed her to get tenure. You must have misheard us."

"Dumb isn't a good look for you," he said.

"Whose side are you on?" I hissed between clenched teeth.

Stupid question, especially considering he was the one with the gun.

Not the only one, it turned out.

Lacey reached into her bag and pulled out a pistol that closely resembled the one clenched in Brad's fist. Seriously, they had mommy-and-me handguns?

Tiffaneigh said, "Brad was just telling us how much you care about him, Lacey. How you'd do anything to help him."

"That's so true. Anything at all. Like how I scheduled a meeting with his professor to convince her there was no need for my poor Bradley to retake her silly class. No one uses Molecular Biology in the real world."

"I want to be an ecologist," Brad muttered. "Scientific knowledge will be useful."

"You can worry about that after you retire from basketball," Lacey said. "Anyway, I went to Professor Zimm's office and demanded she change Brad's grade. Can you believe she refused?"

Tiffaneigh looked like she wanted to say "yes," so I quickly stepped in. "That's so unreasonable."

"Exactly! Athletes shouldn't need to maintain GPAs. She needed to let Brad out before the drop period ended so he could use that extra time to focus on the important thing: basketball."

"I'm never going pro, Mom," Brad protested again. "I just want to play for fun."

"Shut up, darling, you have a gift," Lacey said.

Where were police? If Olive called them when I left Missing Pieces, someone should be here soon. We were across the county line in Willow Falls, but none of the towns around here were that big. I should hear sirens any second.

"How did you get her into the preserve with you?" Tiffaneigh asked.

"Easy. I put a tranquilizer in her coffee. By the time we got to the parking lot, I was practically carrying her already. All I had to do was put her in the passenger seat and go for a drive.

"Listen, girls, I need you to do me a favor. I would love to tell you it doesn't matter how you found out what I did, but the fact is, if you could figure it out, police might also manage. I'd prefer to avoid getting arrested. I've got a facial tomorrow, and it took months to book with this guy."

"It was the coat," Tiffaneigh blurted. "The missing button. Aly saw it when she found the body."

"That's it? One lost button in a sea of black winter coats?" She cocked the gun and pointed it at Tiffaneigh's face. "Aly, why don't you tell me what really happened before I put a bullet in your friend's head?"

My throat seized up. She was right, of course. There was nothing to tell me that button belonged to Brad's coat—except for Olive's psychic powers. Even then, it was my look in the mirror that identified Lacey as the killer rather than Brad.

Neither of those things were proof. I couldn't go to the police with it. I'd never in a million years convince a jury she did anything wrong with that evidence. But now that she'd confessed, I didn't see her letting us walk away.

I couldn't let her shoot Tiffaneigh right in front of me. I also didn't know any way to stop her. With no other options, I blurted out the truth. "I had a vision!"

To my surprise, Lacey burst out laughing. "Oh, dear. That's ludicrous! I'm almost sorry your lie is the last thing poor Tiffaneigh will ever hear."

A gun cocked. My heart lodged in my throat. But it wasn't Lacey's gun.

In one fluid motion, Brad stood, bringing his weapon up to his temple. "Mom. Stop."

Lacey's face turned white. "Brad! What are you doing?"

"Let them go. I mean it. If you hurt either of my friends, I swear, I'll shoot."

"You wouldn't."

"Why not? My mom is a killer. My life has been a lie, with you paying off teachers and threatening people to make things easier for me. Am I even a good basketball player? Or was that a lie, too?"

"Of course you are," she said. "You've got your father's athleticism. Put the gun down. Let us talk about this."

"You first," he said. "Put your gun on the floor. Move away from the door."

When Lacey didn't budge, Brad pressed the gun more firmly against his temple. I thought about twisting his wrist, about stopping him, but fear froze me in place. Part of me didn't believe he'd shoot.

His mom must have, though. She bent her knees an inch at a time until she placed the gun on the floor. Then she pulled herself back up to her full height and took two steps to her left, toward the window. Other than the gun on the ground, the path to the door was clear.

"Tiffaneigh?" Brad said.

"Yeah?"

"Get my mom's gun."

He didn't have to ask her twice. In a heartbeat, she was at the door, gun in her hands. I remained frozen in place, certain if I moved a muscle, someone would get hurt.

"Thanks," Tiffaneigh said. "Aly, let's go."

I glanced at Brad, who nodded his approval. Halfway to the door, I turned back toward him. "Put the gun down."

He sighed but dropped his arm, his shoulders relaxing. Everyone exhaled at the same moment. "It's not loaded."

Lacey let out a sound of outrage and launched herself at Tiffaneigh's knees. Brad lifted his arm and, without hesitation, fired a single shot at his mother. She screamed and fell away from Tiffaneigh, clutching her calf. "You shot me! After everything I did for you?!"

Brad turned a bemused gaze from his mom to the barrel and back. "Huh. Guess it was loaded."

Finally, I heard the welcome sound of sirens in the distance.

Lacey continued to rant and rave, making noises I barely understood. I started to go to her, see if she needed medical attention, but she hissed and lunged at me. A quick jump took me out of harm's way, but she'd have to wait for the paramedics.

Brad sank onto the couch, staring straight ahead. Tears filled his eyes. I couldn't begin to imagine the things going through his head.

"Aly?" Tiffaneigh said from the doorway. "I texted my dad. We can wait for him outside."

I started to follow her, but then I hesitated. After all, he still had a gun. "Brad, are you okay if we leave?"

Outside, sirens wailed. Finally. Either Willow Falls was bigger than I thought or the entire town had decided to drive around the suburbs tonight.

"I guess I'll have to be," he said. "It's time for me to find out who I want to be."

As we reached the front door, two police cars and an ambulance screeched to a halt on the street.

Tiffaneigh's dad burst out of one of them, meeting us on the porch as several other uniformed cops and two EMTs ran through the doorway. Or at least, I assumed that was the dude she ran toward after screaming, "Daddy!" Not knowing what else to do, I stood out of the way and waited for someone to approach.

It didn't take long. Once he assured himself that Tiffaneigh was okay, the man who had to be her father approached. With a start, I realized I'd met him before.

"I'm Detective Pratt," he said. "And you…. Aly, right? Do I know you?"

"You arrested my boss a few weeks ago," I said as realization dawned. "She didn't do it."

"Olive. Right. Sorry about that. We had probable cause."

"Uh-huh." This wasn't the time or the place to rehash that incident, so I changed the subject. "I thought Tiffaneigh said her dad works for the Willow Falls PD."

"He does," she said proudly. "But daddy is so good, they loan him to Shady Grove when Sheriff Matthews needs backup."

"The Shady Grove police budget is small," Detective Pratt said. "Now, why don't you tell me what happened in there?"

By the time we finished relating everything, two paramedics wheeled a screaming Lacey out of the house on a stretcher. An officer followed.

She fought and screeched. "I did it for my baby!"

Poor Brad trailed behind, looking dazed. "I shot her. I shot my mother."

"It was self-defense," Tiffaneigh said. "She was going to kill me and Aly."

"That's right," I said. "You saved us. And your mom is alive."

He shook his head. "They should take me away. It was all my fault."

Detective Pratt said, "Son, if it would make you feel better, we can take you away. I would like you to come down to the station to give a statement. But it seems pretty clear that you saved my daughter and her friend. That's incredibly brave of you."

"Brave? Me?"

Tiffaneigh kissed him on the cheek and looped one arm through his. "That's right. My hero!"

To my surprise, he leaned down and kissed her. Even after experiencing the vision of the two of them together, I'd thought they were just hanging out. Maybe Tiffaneigh was capable of real feelings after all.

Ah, well. Good for them. On that note, it was time for me to head home.

EPILOGUE

AT THE POLICE STATION, Tiffaneigh and I swore up and down that Brad had nothing to do with Professor Zimm's death. We both explained that Lacey had given a full confession. I never mentioned the mirror. When Sheriff Matthews asked me if I knew anything about visions, I told him that killing a woman over her son's grade might suggest Lacey wasn't quite grounded in reality. I felt bad, but the Shady Grove police force wasn't ready to know what I could do. Not yet.

Tiffaneigh texted me later to warn me that she hadn't told anyone about my psychic powers, but she would if I used them to beat her score on the next test. I replied asking if she wanted to be study buddies, only half joking. When she told me she'd decided to stick with Brad, I laughed.

Lacey's car had been meticulously detailed the day after Professor Zimm died, so there was no mud on the outside or DNA evidence. However, the bullet and gun turned out to be a perfect match. Lacey attempted to recant her confession, but with three witnesses to it and the forensic evidence, her lawyer convinced her to plead guilty.

Olive was back to her usual self before Tiffaneigh and I

even met at Brad's. The next day, you couldn't tell there had ever been an issue with her powers. Sam and I reluctantly agreed to reschedule our first date for his next trip to Shady Grove. He respected my need to take our relationship slowly and didn't ask why. We texted every night.

A week later, I went to visit Mary in the rehab facility. To be honest, when I went in and told the front desk who I had come to visit, I expected them to tell me she'd checked out. I still had trouble believing I'd met someone else.

"Tell me something," I said to the woman who led me down the hall to the family room where patients met visitors. "Are patients here allowed to come and go at will?"

"We prefer to call them 'guests' rather than patients," she said. Her name tag identified her as Harmony, a name that fit the rich, gorgeous tone of her voice. Her parents must've been visionaries. "But yes, some of them gain check out privileges after a while. They can leave for short periods of time. This is a voluntary facility. We don't hold anyone against their will."

"Interesting, thanks. Do they have to say where they're going?"

"They don't, but if they come back drunk or high, they lose the privilege."

Hmmm. So maybe Mary had…broken into a rental house to trick me into coming to see her? That still didn't make sense. Why not just call me and invite me here? Or use her own home—Kevin had said she lived in the area before Katrina died. The list of questions I wanted to ask Mary kept getting longer.

We turned a corner, and Harmony led me through a set of French double doors. The room was light and airy, not at all what I'd expected. People sat around watching television, playing chess, or working on other solitary activities. Some sat in pairs chatting. One woman with long honey-colored hair sat in the corner, playing chess by herself. As I watched, she moved a piece, stood up, walked to the other side of the board, made another move, and returned. She even had a time clock.

Warily, I approached. Since I didn't know what I'd find here, I hadn't called in advance (other than to check the visiting hours).

"Mary? You've got a visitor," Harmony said.

The woman looked up and gazed at me without a shred of recognition on her face. She had Katrina's heart-shaped lips and wide-brown eyes. Other than the total absence of warmth in her eyes, she looked exactly like the woman I'd met last week. A good actress?

"Hello," I said. "I'm Kevin's sister. Do you mind if I join you?"

"Do you know how to play chess?"

Not really, but well enough to let her beat me. "I do."

"Then please, have a seat." She gestured to the other side. "It's your turn."

I sat down to study the board, trying to recall how all the pieces moved. Harmony reminded us that lunch was in an hour, then headed back to the front desk. As soon as she passed through the doorway, Mary leaned forward.

"Listen, you've got to help me," she hissed.

"So now you remember me?"

"What?"

"I—" The look of sheer panic on her face stopped me. "Never mind. What do you need?"

"You've got to get me out of here," she said. "I'm not Mary!"

SIGHT SEERING

Buy now!

relax with some family fun at the Shady Grove Annual Treasure Hunt. For twenty-five years, town residents have searched futilely for a chest containing the deed to an abandoned mansion on the edge of town. At this point, Aly's pretty sure the treasure is a myth, but she's always up for Shady Grove shenanigans.

WHEN THE TREASURE Hunt gets underway, a suspicious new resident throws everything into question. Someone's got a hidden motive for participating, and the town may be in danger. Can Aly solve the mystery to save the day?

MYSTIC TREASURE PREVIEW

TODAY WAS the perfect day to win a fortune. I wasn't the only one who thought so: The Shady Grove Town Square hummed with excitement. Fluffy white cumulus clouds peppered the sky. Between the slight breeze and the mercury topping out at seventy degrees, this was the kind of gorgeous summer day that made it worth living through the humidity and thundershowers.

Half the town must have turned out to watch this event. Granted, half the town meant a few thousand people, but still. Town Square was bursting at the seams. Set near the end of Main Street, the largest park in town ran a block down to

Second Street, with the other end across the street from City Hall. My three-year-old nephew and I stood under a tree, soaking it all in while we waited for my brother to join us.

Thankfully, Kyle hadn't yet seen the guy making balloon animals. On the corner nearest me, a marching band warmed up their instruments, complete with a bagpipes player. Town residents milled around, visiting the booths that had been set up to feed and entertain us. A huge banner extended across the square, welcoming everyone to the "WALTER SPARROW ANNUAL MEMORIAL TREASURE HUNT".

According to the rumor mill, Walter Sparrow was some eccentric millionaire who died about twenty-five years ago. Instead of leaving his money to a relative or a friend or a local animal shelter, he created this big annual party for everyone to try to win the big prize. No one had managed yet. My best friend Rusty suspected the entire story was a lie, and Walter just wanted to make sure we all talked about him forever after he passed.

Considering the amount of money supposedly on the line, I was surprised there weren't fortune hunters sniffing around all year, but Shady Grove wasn't like other towns. Maybe the same forces that led to unusual happenings kept outsiders away?

Or maybe our town was so tiny that no one outside a fifty-mile radius had heard of Shady Grove or old Walter? That was more likely.

Personally, I suspected Rusty was right. The whole thing sounded like an urban legend. An excuse for a big summer party, but anyone expecting to find treasure would be sorely disappointed. Still, we'd teamed up and gotten ready for action. The practice solving clues should come in handy once Rusty finished getting his PI license.

Tugging my hand, Kyle peered up at me with his big brown eyes and heart-shaped face from beneath his adorably oversized sun hat. "What's a treasure hunt, Aunt Aly?"

I resisted smoothing an errant chestnut curl that was so like mine. "It means Rusty and I are going to follow clues to find a lost item that has been hidden somewhere in the town."

"I find it! What did Rusty lose?" Kyle asked.

I grinned at the spark of excitement in his eyes and smoothed a curl off of his forehead. My nephew had been born with the power to find lost objects, a secret we preferred to keep from the rest of the world as long as possible. Psychic powers ran in our family, but we'd recently learned that some people wanted to exploit what he could do. "Thanks, Little Man, but this game is for adults only. Besides, in a game, it's not fair to use our special abilities to win."

"Cheating?"

"Yes, that's considered cheating."

"Oh. I won't cheat." Kyle stuck out his lower lip. Then his gaze landed on one of the tables below the "WALTER SPARROW MEMORIAL TREASURE HUNT" banner. "Cookie?"

With a laugh, I let him drag me to the table, manned by my friend and the owner of the local coffee shop, Julie Capaldi. A self-described "recovering lawyer," Julie was a blue-eyed blonde who'd moved to Shady Grove a few years ago to take over her aunt's business. She'd set out cookies for sale, but also—and more importantly—iced coffee.

"Hey! Looking forward to the hunt?" she asked when we got within earshot.

"You know it," I said. "Rusty's excited to practice his PI skills. I'm here to stop him from picking the locks of every store on Main Street."

She laughed. "He's going to be a great investigator. I miss having him at the cafe, though."

Until recently, Rusty had worked as the manager at On What Grounds?. After helping me learn to use my powers and solve a murder, my new best friend discovered his true calling. I often considered myself fortunate Julie hadn't banned me from her store when he left. Where would I get my coffee?

Then again, I suspected she had a thing for my brother.

"Hey, kiddo!" she said to Kyle before offering him a cookie. "You planning to hunt treasure today?"

"Aunt Aly said I was cheating."

My face flamed. Maybe she wouldn't understand him? Three-year-olds didn't have the best enunciation, and his mouth was full of cookie. I wasn't sure how much Julie knew, either about Kyle's abilities or mine. She certainly hadn't heard it from me, but small towns didn't have many secrets.

"Cheating? That's no good." She gave me one of those 'kids say the darnedest things' grins.

In response, I gave her the most innocent look I could muster. "We're learning new words this week. Anyway, are you entering?"

"No, I can't."

"Can't?"

She shook her head and laughed. "I did it last year. You're only allowed to enter once."

"That's odd," I said. "Kevin did it last year, too. I thought he wasn't entering because he wanted to spend the day with Kyle."

"That's part of it, I'm sure. But yeah, everyone gets one chance." She shrugged. "People with money are eccentric, right? It's Walter's estate, so he gets to make the rules. I'll send all my good vibes to you and Rusty."

At the mention of my partner, I turned to scan the crowd. With the pre-hunt festivities drawing to an end, Town Square had cleared out somewhat. A lot of people still stood around, but most moved to ring the center, where the hunt would soon begin.

About fifteen feet away, I spotted my friend Tiffaneigh Pratt talking to Brad Stevens. The three of us studied science together at Maloney College. She still didn't want to admit they were dating, but the two of them looked awfully cozy. Their matching bright blue shirts with "WALTER SPARROW HUNTER" on the back told me everything I needed to know about their relationship—and my primary competition. Tiffaneigh hated to lose, and she had some flexible ideas about what constituted fair and legal gameplay.

We'd need to keep an eye on her if we wanted to win.

Mystic Treasure is ONLY available by signing up for my newsletter - visit www.adabell.com to get your copy.

ACKNOWLEDGMENTS

Thank you again to Tracie Banister for being my muse on this series. Sorry for all the random IMs at weird hours. Thank you to Kara Reynolds, Marty Mayberry, Wendy Ronning, and Sarah Biglow for your feedback. Thank you also for listening to me whine and everything else. Thanks to Victoria Cooper at La Voisin for this beautiful cover. Seriously, I recommend your covers to everyone. Even random people on the street.

I hope you enjoyed this book. If so, please consider leaving an honest review on Bookbub or with your favorite retailer. I love connecting with readers. For access to sneak peeks, advanced access to new releases, and more, please consider supporting me on Patreon.

ALSO BY ADA BELL

Shady Grove Psychic Mysteries

Mystic Pieces

The Scry's the Limit

Sight Seeing

Mystic Treasure (Book 3.5)

Seer Today, Gone Tomorrow

A SHADY GROVE CHRONOLOGY

EVER SINCE ALY moved to Shady Grove, life has been full of surprises. Here's a list of all of Aly's adventures, in chronological order.

<u>MYSTIC PIECES:</u> Aly doesn't believe in psychics. Too bad she just had her first vision. Her first instinct is flat-out denial. After all, science and magic don't mix. But when a man is murdered, Aly realizes that she may be able to use her

strange new "gifts" to find the culprit. If she can avoid getting herself killed in the process.

THE SCRY'S THE LIMIT: Aly's just starting to get the hang of her psychic gifts when she literally stumbles over her favorite professor's body. She's devastated and determined to get justice. But with several people benefitting from Professor Zimm's death, how will Aly find the real culprit before they find her?

SIGHT SEERING: As a psychic who gains powers from antiques, Aly is ecstatic to be invited to an estate sale. It's only after she arrives that she discovers the estate's owner didn't die in her sleep—she was murdered.

MYSTIC TREASURE: Aly and Rusty are excited to participate in the annual Walter Sparrow Treasure Hunt. As the event gets underway, they realize that there's more to this event than meets the eye. Someone's got a hidden motive for participating, and the entire town may be in danger.

THIS NOVELLA TAKES place between the final chapters and epilogue of *Sight Seering*. *Mystic Treasure* is ONLY available by signing up for my newsletter at www.adabell.com. Thank you for hanging out with me!

<u>The Pie in the Scry</u>: After nearly a year, Aly's got a plan to bring Katrina's killer to justice. But before she and Kevin can implement it, she has a vision of someone murdering Tony, the bakery owner. As if that wasn't bad enough—the killer looks exactly like Aly.

<u>Mystic Persons</u>: Aly just completed the biggest spell she's ever attempted, with a little help. But the magic came with an unexpected side effect, and now she's got to figure out why there's a dead man in the bedroom before her parents arrive for their holiday visit.

ABOUT THE AUTHOR

Ada Bell is an award-winning and internationally best-selling author who thought that it would be cool to use a secret identity when writing mysteries. After all, who doesn't want a secret identity? She doesn't remember where the idea for the Shady Grove mysteries started, but she freely admits that Kyle is based on a certain precious toddler in her own life. Ada loves Scooby Doo, superhero movies, STEM heroines, and cake. Mmm, cake.

Find Ada online at www.adabell.com, or get access to sneak peeks, news and more by joining her Facebook group or mailing list.

BOOKS WRITTEN AS LAURA HEFFERNAN

The Reality Star Series

America's Next Reality Star

Sweet Reality

Reality Wedding

The Oceanic Dreams Series

Time of My Life

The Gamer Girls Series

She's Got Game

Against the Rules

Make Your Move

Push and Pole Series

Poll Dancer

The Accidental Senator

Standalone Women's Fiction

Finding Tranquility

Anna's Guide to Getting Even